NATIONAL APPLAUSE
FOR *A PATCH OF BLUE*

"A rare novel to be read . . ."

—TAMPA TRIBUNE

". . . Beautifully and compassionately told . . ."

—CLEVELAND PLAIN DEALER

". . . Absorbing. . ."

—LIBRARY JOURNAL

". . . Powerful and moving . . ."

—NEW YORK TIMES BOOK REVIEW

". . . Excellent . . ."

—WASHINGTON POST

". . . It has vitality, a crusty freshness . . ."

—LOS ANGELES TIMES

"Elizabeth Kata's novel with a voice no bigger than a whisper, shouts great messages that may carry many miles. Compellingly told . . ."

—HARTFORD TIMES

A PATCH OF BLUE

(Original Title: BE READY WITH BELLS AND DRUMS)

by Elizabeth Kata

POPULAR LIBRARY • NEW YORK

CHAPTER ONE

If I hear a person say, 'Man! That's a blue sky—for sure,' I know exactly how the sky looks.

Once, when Rose-ann had asked Ole Pa, 'You like my new dress Daddy-O? Huh?'

Ole Pa had answered her, 'Sure is a fine dress—red as sin. Just fitting for you, Rose-ann.' Ole Pa was shikkered again; drunk and wild.

'Shush! Hush up! You no-good, you—bum . . .'

While Rose-ann lit into Ole Pa I'd sat thinking how good it was to know how the colour of her new dress looked.

If Rose-ann's dress had been black, I'd of known how it looked too. If the dress had been yellow, green or most any other colour, I wouldn't have known.

Times were, I knew how everything looked. But that was before . . .

Before was twelve—no, thirteen years ago. I was turned five. I'm eighteen now.

When I was five, Harry—Rose-ann's husband, my father, came to the room when not expected. He'd been away a long time fighting in a war.

Rose-ann had one of her friends in the room. This made Harry so mad, he up and sliced Rose-ann's friend to a mush.

Even if I hadn't got the acid in my eyes—on my face (by accident: Rose-ann had meant for Harry to be hurt by the acid—not me, but Harry, who was, as I said, unexpected). Even if I hadn't got the acid, I'd never have seen my father again.

The cops came and took Harry away. No one talks about him. It's not fitting to talk about Harry.

I'll always remember the red blood of Rose-ann's friend; clear and bright on the white sheets she had made her bed up with. Made it specially, for her friend.

She is still finicky about fresh white sheets. Her friends appreciate this 'thing' of hers about being so clean. I've heard different friends remark time and again . . .

5

'Sure appreciate this clean love-stack doll . . .' Or words to that effect.

I know blue, because I was for ever looking out of the window when I was small. For ever looking up at the sky. I never got tired of looking at it. So high and clean, way up there. I will never forget blue. That's for sure.

I know red, because red was the last colour (except for black) that I ever saw. Black, I know because it is all I ever see. I love blue. I like red. Black, I hate. I hate everything black.

When I was nine years old, Ole Pa took me out of the room, down the stairs into the street. He took me because one of Rose-ann's friends said:

'Get rid of the kid, doll. I'm no circus performer—get rid of the kid.'

It was strange to be out of the room. I had been out of it so few times since I had been made blind.

Rose-ann and Ole Pa are busy people. Ole Pa, my Grandpa, Rose-ann's old man, works days in a place called 'Mens.' Rose-ann works in the same building, but in a place called 'Ladies.'

At night, to get the smell of 'Mens' out of his system, Ole Pa gets stinking.

Rose-ann has her friends up to the room to 'help out with the high price of things.'

There's no time to spare for taking a person who can't take care of herself—places.

It was crazy to be out of the room. Not cool'n crazy, but scarey'n crazy. The smells were so strong—the noises so many. I couldn't place one of the smells, I couldn't tell what was making the sounds and noise around me—I was frightened.

I sat on the step, waiting, as Ole Pa had told me to. He had gone to get a bottle with the 'pay-off' Rose-ann had given him for taking me out, for clearing the deck.

I was glad when someone spoke.

It made the noises around me not so frightening.

It was a girl who spoke to me.

I told her I was blind and she was nice. She stayed and talked to me. I hadn't talked to a person apart from Rose-ann, Ole Pa, or some of Rose-ann's friends, for so long. It was fine!

The girl said maybe we could be friends. Maybe she could

come up to the room, tell me things. Maybe she could even bring me down to sit on the steps sometimes. Tell me what everything looked like.

Her name was Pearl. I liked her name. I liked her voice. I seemed to have a new life opening up.

I was mad with Ole Pa when he came back. When he came back he said:

'Scat!'

Just like that. 'Scat!'

I was disappointed and mad.

'Why did you say "scat" just like that—why did you send my friend away?'

'Your friend!' said Ole Pa. 'Your friend was a nigger!'

'I don't care. I don't care.' I cried. Then I asked him. 'What is a nigger like? Why can't I have a nigger friend?'

'Niggers is black.' Ole Pa told me. 'You want to have a black friend? That one was black as night.'

Black! I hated Pearl. I had enough black in my life.

If only Pearl had been red—or blue . . .

CHAPTER TWO

Every inch of the room we live in I know as well as I know the teeth inside my mouth. Just like my tongue knows the number and shape of my teeth, that's how well I know the room.

I keep it as neat as a pin. Rose-ann has taught me how to do this. If Ole Pa so much as moves a thing an inch, I know.

When I was small I had to wait till one of them came home before I could eat, but I learnt to get the food ready and I like to eat before they come in. Because both Rose-ann and Ole Pa work in the place they do, when they first come home everything about them smells of disinfectant and I hate the smell of disinfectant.

I eat first; they eat when they come in. Times are, they don't come in all night. So, as Rose-ann says,

'It's a good thing the kid's smart.'

'It's a crying shame the kid's smart.' Ole Pa just *has* to go against everything, but everything. He can't help it. It's the way he is.

'Says you. A skid row drunk like you . . .'

Rose-ann and Ole Pa just have to quarrel and disagree. It's the way they are.

'Says me.' Ole Pa thumped his fist on the table. This is a habit of his. Times are I've leapt high into the air from the unexpectedness of those thumps of his.

'Says you, says you, says a dirty old bum like you—hoo hoo!' Rose-ann laughed.

Thump! 'Says me. Better—now she's a big girl—maybe better Sleena was dead,' Ole Pa yelled at her. 'Better dead!'

'Better a bum like you was dead. Now that's an idea! Sleena has a good life. Nice and quiet. Nice and clean.' Rose-ann was good and mad with Ole Pa. 'Anything wrong with your life, Sleena?' Sometimes Rose-ann becomes very high tone.

Thump! 'Sleena has a whale of a time. Your life's just dandy—ain't it, Sleena?' Ole Pa and Rose-ann never talk much to me—only times like this when they are fighting, then they fire questions at me.

I think over what they ask me. I think seriously, because I want to give a good answer to their questions and because I'm glad to have them take an interest in me.

They never give me time to make an answer. The few times I've managed to slip one in, they've ignored me.

The worst, but the worst fight Rose-ann and Ole Pa ever had, was the night one of her friends—not a regular—a casual, locked Rose-ann out of the room and did me over. That was a bad night for me, for sure.

I had always thought Rose-ann was having a good time for herself on that clean bed of hers! From that night on I knew different and I began to admire Rose-ann for her bravery and I took notice of her oft-repeated remark that:

'No broad, no broad, worked tougher for a bit of extra, than Rose-ann D'arcey.'

That night I thought Ole Pa was going to make a mush of Rose-ann, the way Harry'd made mush of her former friend, the night he'd come home unexpected from the war.

Ole Pa blew his top.

Rose-ann, as she explained, was not to blame. She was mad at her friend's behaviour. But, as she said:

'What—locked out there in the hall—could I do? Tell me? I'm open—but wide—to suggestions.'

Ole Pa laid into Rose-ann. No one could tell about this fight. It had to be heard to be believed. A bad fight.

From that night on, Rose-ann changed towards me. She began to hate me. I was sad for she's always been rather nice to me.

From that night she rented a room down the hall and there she invited her friends. For that I was glad.

It was a small room, with no window at all. Rose-ann said it wasn't so bad in cold weather, but—hot times—wow! In hot times the room was bad, Rose-ann said, and bad for business. No guy like to have his guts steamed out of him!

Rose-ann told Ole Pa and me: 'No guy wants to have his guts steamed out a him! That I was told last night—by a regular too.'

'Rose-ann doll,' he said. 'My guts is clean steamed out a me. Get in touch doll, when you get air conditioning, huh!'

'How 'bout that! Me, Rose-ann, given the breeze. How 'bout that? A regular gives me the breeze. Why? My own kid—own kid mind you—ogles one of my friends, breaks into my business. How 'bout that, huh!'

Rose-ann was mad. Ole Pa thumped.

'Sleena never ogled no friend of yours, Rose-ann.'

'And I say she did.' Rose-ann was getting madder.

'Rose-ann, sure as hell, sure as hell, you have a black heart,' said Ole Pa. 'Sleena here, can't ogle. Sleena's—blind.'

'Hoo hoo! You tellin' me?'

'Can it,' yelled Ole Pa. 'Hush your mouth. Lay off Sleena. You love your business. Lay for a buck anytime, anywhere, you would, and you do . . .'

'A buck! Me?' Rose-ann screamed at Ole Pa.

'Yeah, you. Big mouth,' bawled Ole Pa.

'Dirty dirty dirty—listen to the dirtiest lowest bum talking. What *you* wouldn't do for a buck . . . Hoo hoo!'

Ole Pa hated more than anything being called dirty. He hated dirt. I thought there was going to be trouble between Rose-ann and Ole Pa. We all hate dirt.

The worst thing about being blind, the very worst—is not being able to see if things are clean or not. Food! Take food. Often I've thrown out food it's taken me for ever to prepare. Wrapped it up, dumped it in the trash can, just in case perhaps a fly crawled over it. Perhaps a dead insect had fallen into it. Oh my God! I wish at times I get to thinking these things—I wish I could see . . .

Rose-ann told Ole Pa he was just about the lowest, the dirtiest bum she had ever in all her years seen.

'In all my thirty-five years of life,' said Rose-ann in her high-tone voice, 'I have never seen no dirtier bum than you, my own father.'

Instead of things blowing up, they didn't. Ole Pa forgot about being called dirty because he became mad at Rose-ann for putting her age back ten years.

Another thing that makes Ole Pa wild is lies.

They had a fine fight about Rose-ann's age. I waited until she had gone down the hall to the room where one of her friends was disturbing residents of the building, banging and calling out very rude wild words.

I heard her yelling at her friend, yelling at some of the residents who were complaining.

After she had banged the door of the room shut on her friend and herself, I asked Ole Pa if he would like to stay a while and play a game of dominoes with me before he went out to get stinking.

Ole Pa said he just couldn't think of anything worse than playing dominoes with a blind tomato.

All he wanted to do was to get stinking, shut of both Rose-ann and me.

I was sorry he felt like that. I had vainly, as often before, hoped that he, because of his taking my side against Rose-ann, might have done it because he liked me.

Before Ole Pa went out I asked him if Rose-ann really had a black heart.

'Does Rose-ann really have a black heart, Ole Pa?' I asked.

'Yes, Rose-ann has a black heart,' Ole Pa told me.

'What colour is your heart, Ole Pa?' I prayed to God above that his wouldn't be black too.

'My heart?'

'Yes. What colour is your heart, Ole Pa?'

'What colour do you like best now?'

'I like blue best, Ole Pa.'

'That's the colour of my heart—blue.'

'Blue!' I was glad. 'Do you know the colour of my heart, Ole Pa?' I made up my mind that if mine was black, somehow I would kill myself. I waited, hardly breathing, to see if he knew.

'Your heart is white, Sleena.' Ole Pa opened the door to the hall.

I remembered that I knew another colour. White! I was excited.

'Do you think there is also some red in my heart, as well as white?'

'Would you like that, Sleena?'

'Yes.'

'Then there is.'

'For sure?'

'For sure. Now hush up.' And Ole Pa went out to get drunk. I was glad his heart was blue and that mine was red and white. I knew I never could bear to have Rose-ann with her black heart touch me or do anything for me again.

CHAPTER THREE

The best day of the week to me is the day Mr Faber comes to take away the work I do for him, the day he leaves new work for me to do.

For years and years—for ever and for ever—I've strung beads on threads for Mr Faber.

I guess there's nothing really hard about threading beads. Come to think of it, there is nothing hard. Grading is the tricky part.

Mr Faber brings his beads in seven boxes. Each box rattles with different-sized beads: thousands of beads. Everyone has a tiny hole through which I pass the thread. I—so Mr Faber says—should be proud of my record. Never have I made a mistake, never lost a bead . . .

Mr Faber comes from a place called Poland. He is gentle and I like listening to his soft voice. When he leaves me I try to sound like him. To talk the way he does. I have to move my mouth and my tongue in the strangest ways. This has always made me laugh. I can speak exactly the same way that Mr Faber speaks.

'Arnd ow wis moi bust vorker do-day?' It always makes me laugh.

Sometimes he brings his dog with him. No one could ever understand my feelings about Mr Faber's dog. I love that dog. If that dog belonged to me I know I would feel proud, but *proud*.

I am always disappointed that Mr Faber can't change his dog's name. I've asked, no, pleaded with him many times about it. Scum-dorg! That's the name of the best dog to ever live in this world.

'Please, Mr Faber, won't you change the name for me, your best and most faithful worker? Never one bead graded wrongly or gone astray. That's what you say yourself. Please?'

I know he has tried; I've heard him trying.

'No,' he always says. 'No. I vish dart I cout. I carnt.'

I've called that dog a dozen different fine names. He only answers to Scum-dorg.

Mr Faber, during our many chats over the years, has always said:

'I say it is a vicked zin. You zhould get out in the zunzhine, get out to zit in bark.'

He has told me so much about the park that I feel I know it as well as the room, almost.

It was three weeks before I won him over to taking me there.

The air in the park—so sharp and clean. The floor of the park! Mr Faber laughed and laughed. He laughed because I pulled my shoes off and there I was, standing under the blue sky, breathing the clean sweet air, my feet in the cool damp grass. I laughed, I laughed for happiness. I began to ask Mr Faber question after question. He answered them all. Oh God! How I wish I could remember what 'green' looked like. Nearly all Mr Faber's answers had 'green' in them.

Practically all the knowledge I have, just about everything I know, I learnt from listening to the radio. Sometimes I surprise myself at all the things I know. For example: I know that the Tower of London is an ancient fortress, palace and prison. Covers thirteen acres. One of its oldest structures, White Tower, built 1078-80. Has three storeys, exterior walls fifteen feet thick, etc. etc.

I know that Asama-Yama is a volcanic mountain in Japan, that it overlooks the village where the Crown Prince of

Japan played tennis and fell in love with the girl he has married.

I know that the Island of Sumatra is the sixth largest island in the world—1,115 miles long, 275 miles across. I know that a tarpon is a South Atlantic fish which affords good sport for anglers off the coast of Florida.

I know many, many things, I never forget what I hear, and yet! Green? I don't know green.

That first wonderful day in the park! I just could not go back to the room. Not yet.

At first Mr Faber was understanding and patient, but in the end he became grumpy. This, naturally, I could understand.

Mr Faber has many dependants, everyone of them depending on him for their daily bread. Grandma Faber is 97 years old and little Spigniff arrived only six weeks ago. There is Mrs. Faber, and many others as well.

'Five more minutes, five minutes more,' I begged.

'No.'

Back in the room my hands were unsteady. I couldn't keep my promise to Mr Faber to 'vork vaster.'

I knew I could never be satisfied to sit in the room day after day. I must—for sure—go to the park again.

I gave up trying to work.

CHAPTER FOUR

Before Rose-ann left for 'Ladies' the following morning, by a stroke of bad luck she knocked over one of the bead boxes. I heard the rattle rattle as they spilt over the floor.

I loved the sound they made, but I was sorry that Rose-ann knew they were not, as usual, all strung on their strings ready for Mr Faber.

Rose-ann let fly. Ole Pa let fly.

I had been hoping that I could explain to Mr Faber how I had let him down, broken my fine record. I almost had confidence that he would leave the money for Rose-ann in full amount. I was going to promise him to work double quick with the new lot.

Rose-ann hadn't slapped me since I was about twelve, and then she had only done so when justified. Like the time I was sick over the clean bed, the time I let the supper burn to a crisp, careless things. This time, though, it was different.

I thought my head was going to roll on the floor and keep company with Mr Faber's unstrung beads. Rose-ann has a mighty powerful pair of arms and hands.

'Leave be—leave Sleena be—you lousy tart.'

Suddenly Ole Pa began to take my side. I almost wished he hadn't. It was good not to be hit any more, but the yelling made me feel worse than ever.

'Hoo-hoo!' Rose-ann turned on Ole Pa. Once more I can't describe the words and way they carried on.

A resident from over the hall banged on our door and said if we couldn't lay off the racket the cops would sure be able to quieten us. Both Rose-ann and Ole Pa have a strong dislike of connecting with the cops. They quietened down considerably.

During the quiet, I spoke my piece. I said that Mr Faber, on my asking, had taken me to the park. I knew full well that Mr Faber was safe from attack, because God knows it's hard enough to find a way for a shiftless blind girl to earn money. I knew no harm would come to him.

'If you don't let me go to the park I will never string another bead on another string,' I finished up. I think I felt proud at that moment; anyways, I felt brave.

On the third day of no beads on strings. No supper cooked. No cleaning done. On that day Ole Pa and Rose-ann gave in. Not gave in easy, but gave in.

' . . . and just how do you plan to get there?' Ole Pa asked me flatly.

Just as flatly, I told him: 'You can drop me there on your way to "Mens." '

' . . . and how, just howah do you intend to do your beads, theah in the pawk?' Rose-ann asked.

Jesus, the beads! I'd made no plans of how I could manage my work. Quick as a quiz-kid I answered.

'I'll take a small rug with me and take my boxes. I'll work double quick time out there in the park.' I spoke clear and firm. 'If I don't do just double my quota the first week, if I don't, I'll give up the idea,' I promised, using the tone of voice girls on radio plays use when they are taking 'him' for better or for worse.

'I promise. I do,' I added.

'Why you no good, you lousy little slacker, holding out on your work all this time.' I felt the tiny breeze Rose-ann's hand made as she raised it to crack me one again. I dipped my head, quick as the click of a light switch.

'Enough of that, slut. Leave Sleena be.' Ole Pa and Rose-ann did a quick shuffle.

'O.K. O. Kay!' Rose-ann sat on the bed. I know that Rose-ann has got a lot fatter lately because when she sits on the bed these days it makes much more noise than of yore. 'I'm against the entire set-up,' said Rose-ann. 'The entire set-up is ridiculous. Who, who is going to clean, cook, do the little things that have to be done, always have been done by Sleena? Little enough, indeed, for all the benefits she, Sleena has received. Who is going to do all these little things? If I dare to arsk?'

'I will still do them. Do them better'n ever.' My voice was deeper than I had ever heard it. I couldn't believe it was my voice.

'Do them better'n ever,' I repeated.

'When, pray?' asked Rose-ann.

'I'll get up earlier. I'll stay up longer.'

'I want my supper at the time I'm used to.' Rose-ann, I knew, was pouting out her lips, speaking sulky. I knew, because I always copy the way people sound and to sound sulky one pouts out one's lips. It's the only way to sound good and sulky.

'Hush up! Put a tuck in your greedy mouth.' Ole Pa was coming strongly to my side against Rose-ann.

'Perhaps,' I said with cunning. 'Perhaps I had better give up the idea. Rose-ann works harder'n any of us. She *needs* her supper on time.' I waited hopefully.

'Big—fat—slob,' said Ole Pa. 'Blubber-belly on the bed there.'

'Hoo-hoo!' Rose-ann got off the bed. 'Listen to beer-belly. Listen to the greasy old tub of lard talking about blubber, talking about fat bellies.'

'Hush up,' repeated Ole Pa. 'You can wait a bit for your supper. Only one thing messing up your idea, Sleena. Only one thing stops the business. And it's not fatso's supper.' Ole Pa was putting in his top denture, I heard the click it made against his bottom teeth and I heard the way he sucked air through them—'tsk-tsk-tsk . . .' He only wore his denture when he went out. He was leaving. Nothing settled, and he was leaving.

'Tsk-tsk—two things, Sleena,' said Ole Pa. 'Stop you from spendin' your days in the fresh green park.'

'What?' I asked, and my heart beat so slow and throbbing I thought for sure it was going to stop.

'What *are* these two things?' I asked again.

'First thing,' said Ole Pa, 'no one to bring you home to the room.'

'You can bring me. I can wait, I don't mind how late . . .'

'It will be good and dark; many a time I'm not on my way home till good and dark,' said Ole Pa.

Was that all? 'Dark is nothing, but nothing to me, I'm always in the dark.' I was near to crying.

Ole Pa was silent so long, then: 'How 'bout that! So you are. How 'bout that, Rose-ann? Sleena's always in the dark.' He sure sounded surprised.

'So what?' asked Rose-ann; still sulky.

'So what!' I echoed. 'Who cares about the dark? Not me.'

'Always in the dark,' muttered Ole Pa. It seemed to be preying on his mind.

'I'm used to it,' I told him.

Rose-ann had begun to make up her face. I smelt the scent of her foundation cream, the sickly smell of her face-powder. She spoke to Ole Pa.

'Tell Sleena the other reason, the real reason. The reason we don't parade her through the streets. Go on, blabbermouth, tell her.' I knew she was doing her lips by the sound of her voice. I have never done my lips, but if I stretched my lips, closed my teeth, I could sound just as she sounded when she talked during the putting on of her mouth.

'Tell me, Ole Pa?' I had to know.

'Your face—ain't sightly,' said Ole Pa.

Not sightly? I felt sad, as sad as Mr Faber had sounded the day he told me one of his children had died.

'Not sightly? In what way not sightly, Ole Pa?'

'It got marked with the acid. The night Harry . . .'

'I know about that. Is my face bad to look at? Is it, Ole Pa?' Why hadn't I known about this before?

'Not bad. But—not good, Sleena.' Ole Pa sounded old and tired. I was sorry for him.

'Is it real bad, Rose-ann?' I asked Rose-ann.

'Your face is a lousy mess,' said Rose-ann. Now, *she* had

given me this face. Not, mind you, on purpose; this I had always known. But I was sad again, because her voice didn't sound one whit sorry that she, by accident, had made a lousy mess of my face.

Rose-ann went on to say that she, for one, had had enough of crazy business. Subject was closed, finished.

'Forget about the park, Sleena. Think of all the benefits you have—forget about the park.'

'No,' I said. 'If my face is so lousy, I shall wear one of your hats—one with a veil.'

'Hoo hoo hoo! Hah hah hah hah hah . . .' Rose-ann was laughing as though she was fit to be tied.

'You're killing me. Stop it, you're killing me,' laughed Rose-ann. 'You—one of my hats. Hah hah hah.'

'Get ready to go to the park, Sleena,' said Ole Pa. 'You don't need a hat. You don't need any of Rose-ann's trappings. Get ready.'

'Now?' I asked.

'Now.'

Suddenly I was frightened at the thought of going to the park. It would be strange. Full of people. Strange people. They would look at me. Laugh at the sight of a shiftless blind girl sitting on a rug threading beads. Maybe it would rain. Thunder! I was scared of thunder. When it thundered, I crawled under the bed. What if a storm came? Out there—alone?

Maybe a cop would tell me to 'move on' because my mess of a face was making people in the park feel sick. I had better by far stay in the room. I was sick with disappointment. So that they would not know why I had changed my mind, after causing such a rhubarb, I pretended concern about Mr Faber.

'I think I had better not go today. Mr Faber! I must explain to Mr Faber. I must pick up the beads. (How was I to find all the spilt beads? It would take hours.) I must be here for Mr Faber,' I said.

'That's about it,' said Rose-ann. 'Have supper on time, Sleena. I've a heavy night ahead.' Rose-ann banged the door shut. I heard her footsteps, tip tap tip, as she went down the hall.

'Don't worry about Mr Faber. I'll explain to Mr Faber.' I could hardly believe my ears. Ole Pa was sweeping the beads into a pile, rattling them into a box.

'Pack a lunch, Sleena,' said Ole Pa. 'I have to be on my way. I haven't all day you know. I have a job you know. I have to be on time you know. Get moving.'

'Yes. Yes, yes. Pack a lunch.' I put some crackers into a paper bag. 'Lunch packed,' I said.

'Now, I can't do this every day.' Ole Pa was becoming angry, impatient.

'Every day!' I laughed, not a happy laugh, or a laugh for something funny—but a laugh thin and silly.

'Certainly not, Ole Pa, not every day. Just today and—sometimes,' I said. I was shaking, every inch of me was shaking like mad. 'I'm all ready, Ole Pa,' I said.

'Aren't you going to get dressed?' asked Ole Pa in a shocked voice.

'Dressed?' I was still barefoot, still in my pyjamas. I laughed. Ole Pa laughed too. We laughed together. It sounded good.

'Better get dressed,' laughed Ole Pa.

'Yes,' I said. I pulled my curtain closed and while I put on my undies I talked to Ole Pa. 'What shall I wear? I haven't much choice. Come and choose for me, Ole Pa.'

I was trying him too far. I should've known.

'Wear anything,' shouted Ole Pa. 'Wear anything.'

'Yes, yes, anything.' How did I look? Did I look a mess? Would everything about me be as messy as my loused-up eyes and face? I wished I knew. God! I wished I could see.

I was sweating wet. Sweating wet and sick, shaking in every inch of me, when at last I was sitting with my back against the trunk of a tree. Sitting on my rug. Sitting with my seven small bead boxes in front of me. My thread box on my knee. I breathed deeply. The air was as sweet as I remembered. The air was wonderful. I began to feel grand and excited again, when Ole Pa dropped a shocker, a downright stinker on me.

'Sleena?' said Ole Pa.

I knew by his voice that something was amiss.

'What?' I whispered. I couldn't bear anything to go wrong now. 'What is it?' I asked.

'Sleena. How you going to manage about—you know what?' asked Ole Pa.

'You know what' was the way Ole Pa spoke of people's private needs. Even when I was very small Ole Pa never came straight out and said: 'You've wet your pants.' Always

he would say, 'There! You've done—you know what again.'
In some ways he is a most polite man.

The question bowled me over. I knew a lot of things. I
could answer many a question. I'm sure I could win one of
those big-money quiz competitions. If Ole Pa had asked me:
'Sleena, what is a Dhole?' Snap! I could've answered right off,
'A Dhole is a wild dog found in India.' I could've answered a
million questions almost. But I had no answer for the one he
had asked.

'I never figured on that,' I said slowly.

'No,' said Ole Pa. 'I suppose not.'

He waited as though for sure I was going to come through
with a smart solution.

'No idea?' he asked at last.

'I just won't,' I said.

'You're only human,' said Ole Pa.

'Don't give it another thought, Ole Pa. I just won't.'

'I've got to go. Sleena you sit exactly here. You are not to
move one inch. You hear me?'

'I hear you,' I said. 'I'll be just here. Just like this. I promise. And—Ole Pa?'

'Yes.'

'Thank you, Ole Pa.'

He didn't answer me.

'Ole Pa? Thank you—for being so nice to me. I hope you
won't get trouble for being late at "Mens." I will be just here
as you see me now. I promise. And, Ole Pa? Is my face
really, no kidding, as loused-up as Rose-ann says?'

Still he didn't answer.

'Ole Pa?'

I knew that he had gone. I was alone—and scared so that I
could have died.

CHAPTER FIVE

I settled back against the trunk of the tree. I would just sit
awhile.

I heard a million small sounds I had never heard before:

magic teasing sounds. The dearest sound I heard was made
by a leaf—it fell on top of my head—ff . . t . .

I put up my hand to see what it was, because I had not
known that it was a leaf. Good little leaf to fall from your
branch in summer instead of waiting for the autumn. Falling
just to make me happy.

I felt along the curving centre vein of the leaf—my first
leaf.

I counted the uneven scallops. Eleven, and one ungrown,
little scallop.

The centre vein was like a great river, with little rivers
branching out. On the back of my leaf, the centre vein was
raised, like the back one of a fish.

I found out later that my leaf fell from an oak tree. I
would've loved it no matter where it came from.

That morning in the park, every bird sang, like mad.

Crazy, cool little winds danced over the grass and carried
the loveliest smells I had ever smelt.

It was hard to sit still. I wanted to jump up, pull off my
shoes. I wanted to climb to the very tip top of my tree. Roll
on the grass. Hunt for the flowers that I knew must be
somewhere near. But as Rose-ann is always saying: 'The milk
has been spilt. You're blind, Sleena. No use crying.'

So I sat, as Ole Pa had told me, but you can take a long
shot on the fact that my heart and mind were dancing like
mad.

I knew I should be doing beads. But how could I?

I just sat.

My conscience but jumped when I heard a far-away clock
striking eleven. I couldn't believe I had been in the park for
more than two hours!

I threaded my needle.

In the room I had always been able to thread without
knowing I was threading. Out here in the park it was
different. So many things to take my mind away from my
hands.

Something else, not a leaf, fell from the tree, down the
neck of my blouse. I felt it creeping down, down. Horrible!
I tried to reach it with my hand and knocked over one of the
bead boxes.

There was a slope where I was sitting.

That was that!

I would not be able to come to the park any more. I could

never find all those beads in the grass. I hadn't even one thread completed. Not even one thread. It was too sad—more than sad.

I felt finished. The milk—no, the beads had been spilt—for sure.

No use to say 'no use to cry.' I sat and cried.

When Gordon asked me, 'Can I do anything to help you?' I stopped crying.

I covered my face with my hands and listened with all of me.

'Are you all right?' asked Gordon.

I found out later that Gordon had been sitting on a bench when Ole Pa and I had arrived at the tree. He'd been watching me for more than two hours. Just watching.

See how bad it is to be unable to see!

He had watched me play with my oak leaf, listen to the sounds around me, begin my work, knock over the box—watched me cry.

Gordon's voice was so deep that although it came from above me it seemed to come from all about me. Almost I thought it was the tree saying, 'ARE—YOU—ALL—RIGHT?'

I took away my hands. I knew that the owner of the voice would not mind my unsightly face. I knew I should've said, this being a stranger, 'Thank you. Nothing is wrong.'

But I felt free to say: 'Yes. Something is wrong. I've spilt a box of beads. I'm blind. I can't do my work without I find every one.'

'I thought you were blind,' said Gordon. 'I've been watching you. Now let me see—beads, beads, ah—yap! Dozens of the little devils.'

I heard them dropping into the box.

It was hard to believe my luck. 'I thank you from the depths of my heart,' I said. I spoke in my deepest voice.

For the first time I heard Gordon laugh. I never heard anyone laugh like that before—warm. Comforting.

'You are a honey,' said Gordon. 'There! Every bead back in the box ma'm—what happens now?'

'Now?' I asked.

'Yes. What do you do with the beads?' He was picking them up, letting them rain back—pak, pak, pak—into the box.

'Grade and thread them on these.' I showed him the threads.

'Does it take long? How clever you are. Do you ever make mistakes?'

'Clever! Even a fool couldn't make a mistake.'

'So easy even a blind person can do it, huh?'

The way Gordon said 'blind' made it sound like something not to be hidden away.

'Yes,' I said. I laughed, and I liked the sound of my laugh, so I laughed again.

'Do you come here often?' he asked. 'I come here every day. I've never seen you before.'

'Because I've come for the first time today. That's why you've never seen me.' Then I asked him, 'Why do you come here every day? Sir,' I added politely.

'I work at night. I work for a newspaper. Usually I don't come to the park until much later. Something got into me this morning. Go to the park early, this 'thing' said. I was quite angry—having to get up earlier, rushing down to the park. Now I know that I came because you would need me to find your beads. Wonderful, isn't it, the way things work out!'

It took him a long time to say all that because he spoke each word clear; each word had a beginning and an end, not like Rose-ann, Ole Pa and me. We speak so fast each word trips over the next.

'And,' he went on speaking, 'you must not call me Sir. My name is Gordon Ralfe—I'm a man just six feet tall, aged thirty—I served in the Navy. I———'

'Excuse me, Mr Ralfe,' I interrupted. 'I'm not used to meeting new people. I am sure pleased to meet you. You are telling me so much all at once. May I ask how much taller than me six feet is?'

'How tall *are* you? Hmmm! I should say you would be five feet, yes, and perhaps four inches, so I must be just about eight inches taller than you. Next question, please?'

No one had ever allowed me the freedom of asking questions—allowed me, *asked* me to ask! I thought deeply. The thing about my face being unsightly was uppermost, so I asked:

'Would you kindly tell me. Is my face—I know I have a loused-up face— I know that, Mr Ralfe, but is it—does it make you . . . ?' I wished I had not asked about myself. He, I supposed, was disappointed that my question was not about him, for he did not seem to want to answer me. Then he said:

'Loused up? Your face! Loused up? If you wore dark glasses—if you did—you'd be one of the prettiest girls in the world. I know this because I've been all over the world.'

'All over the world?' I gasped. I couldn't believe it.

Gordon laughed again. 'I see one has to be careful talking to you. Not exactly all over the world, but places, I've been places, have surely seen, as I was saying when so rudely interrupted'—I knew he was smiling—'a mighty lot of pretty gals. You, with dark glasses, would be one of them.'

'How come?' I couldn't believe him. I wanted to but I couldn't. Sleena—pretty? I'd always loved that word.

'How come? I'll be your mirror. Now, let me see . . . Pale gold hair. Pale gold skin. Nose fit for an angel. Why, your face is a perfect little heart. It's not often one sees a girl with a face shaped like a perfect little heart.'

'Isn't it?' I didn't want to disappoint him by saying that I'd no idea what an angel's nose was like, or that pale gold was something I knew nothing of. It sounded very nice, every thing about me sounded very nice.

'It surely is not,' he said. 'It's most unusual.'

'You didn't tell me about . . .' I began. He knew what I meant.

'About your eyes? I was coming to that. Your eyes don't matter.'

'Don't matter?'

'Don't matter. What happened to them?'

I told him about Harry. About Rose-ann and the acid she had meant for Harry but which, instead, by accident, I had got.

'Too bad. Could've been much worse though. The acid spoilt your eyesight. It made it so that you have no eyelashes, and the acid burnt a few holes into the nice skin about your eyes. Not bad though. Dark glasses will fix all that.'

'Will?' What was he saying?

'You must get them at once. I wear them. Millions of people wear them.'

'Why?'

'To stop the sun being so bright. To hide behind. You have no idea how many people wear dark glasses to hide behind.'

'You?' I asked.

'I'm one of the hiders. I wear them so I will not have to show people my true feelings. I also wear them because many people look nicer to me through them.'

'Why don't you want people to see your true feelings, Mr Ralfe?'

'My true feelings would sometimes make people angry. When people get angry, trouble starts.'

That—for sure—I knew! Take Harry, for instance.

'You see what I mean about dark glasses?' Gordon asked.

'No,' I said. 'I don't *see*. But I understand.' I'd made a joke. I laughed. I'd never laughed so much before.

'As well as having a heart-shaped face, you are a very nice girl. I like you very much. When I like people I like to be able to call them by their name.' He sat down beside me. I heard the heels of his shoes squeak on the grass.

'My name is Sleena,' I told him. 'Sleena D'arcey.' He was silent, then he said, 'Sleena! What a poor sounding name that is. Are you sure your name is Sleena?'

I was sorry I had told him my name. I wished I had told him my name was Angela, Ingrid—any name but Sleena.

'That's my name.' Man! I was sorry I'd told him my name.

'Sleena! It's awful. How do you spell it?'

'S-e-l-i-n-a.' I spelt out my name.

'Selina! Selina—that is a beautiful name. Why do you mutilate it? Why do you make such a beautiful name sound so ugly. Don't ever do it again. Now! Let's do it all over again. I'll ask you, and you will say, you know what you will say. Here goes. What is your name fair lady?' asked Gordon.

'My name—is—Selina.' Sounded nice for sure.

'How do you do—Selina,' said Gordon. 'But you should have said: "My name is Selina, Gordon." Perhaps you don't like my name?'

'I do. I like your name, it is a deep name. I like it.'

'Then say it.'

'Gordon,' I said.

'That's fine,' said Gordon. 'Now that we know each other's names, heights, and so on, perhaps you will allow me to help you do the beads. I could grade them, have them all ready for you to thread . . . How about that? Huh?'

The beads. Jesus! The air in the park was making me 'shikkered'—I was shikkered with the air of the park, like liquor shikkers Ole Pa.

I knew it was mad to be like this. I should've said: 'Please don't trouble.' But I said: 'Cer-razy man, cer-razy. When does we start?'

'Now,' laughed Gordon. 'We start right now.'

It was fun. I'd never had fun before. We never stopped talking for one second. No sooner would one string be finished than another started.

Gordon was telling about the time when he was doing Service in Japan; how, being six feet tall, every time he went to eat or visit in a Japanese style room he cracked his head on the low door tops. I was laughing because he made it sound very funny. 'Ouch! done it again. Ouch! Man! I was black and blue. Selina, I tell you I bumped my head so many times I was black and blue. You are a cruel girl to laugh.'

'Oh Gordon, no,' I said. 'Not black 'n blue. Only blue—or blue'n red. Not black . . . please not black.' I wasn't laughing any more.

'Why not?' he asked.

I told him about Pearl. I told him about Rose-ann's heart, about how I hated, hated all things black. 'Please say only blue, or red and blue.'

'Let's just say—then, let us just say—Gordon Ralfe received a continuous series of painful bumps, which caused lumps, and which caused him to utter many and varied blasphemous and rude words,' said Gordon. 'What shall we do now?'

'Do now?' I asked in surprise.

'Now that we have completed today's quota of beads . . .'

'Completed? They can't be all done. Three days I'm back.' I was scared for sure. Had he perhaps stolen some of the beads? I was wicked to think this. It was impossible that three days' work had been done already. 'I must count the completed strings—there must be—there should be——' I could hardly speak for nerves.

'There are ninety,' said Gordon. 'Here, I have packed them in this box. Is that O.K.?'

I felt the box. I knew by its weight that there were ninety strings of beads. I wanted to cry. I was ashamed, I still couldn't believe they were all done. Three days' hard work done in——

'What time is it, Gordon?' I asked.

'Past lunch-time. What would you like for lunch, Selina D'arcey? Would you care for Suki-Yaki? Hungarian goulash? Would you care for pheasants' tongues? Perhaps you fancy . . .'

'Please, Gordon.' I don't know why everything he said made me laugh. Made me feel light and happy. It was not really what Gordon said; it was his way of saying things.

'Well?' he asked.

'I've got my lunch,' I told him. I showed him my bag of crackers.

'Strictly for the birds! Crackers are for the birds.' He threw my crackers high into the air. I heard the movement of his arm as he threw. 'We, being human, rate better than crackers. I know a place near by. Spring-rolls! Do you like Chinese Chow, Selina?'

'Love that Chinese Chow,' I told him. I had never eaten Chinese Chow. He left me alone. When he was gone I leant once more against the tree. I held my leaf against my cheek. I loved that little old leaf. I was excited, so happy. For the first time in my life of eighteen years, someone had talked, laughed, helped me. I was trembling for happiness.

What if Gordon didn't come back? What if he just had gone off—never came back? He had been away a long time. He had said 'Just close by.' He wasn't coming back. Well, I would remember this day as the happiest in my life—for sure.

The grass was thick and soft but I heard him coming. I felt him sitting beside me. I was so glad I couldn't move.

He sat still. I realized that Gordon thought maybe I was asleep. Was it, perhaps, not Gordon? Was it perhaps a bad person? I couldn't see, I didn't know. God! I wanted to be able to see.

'Gordon?' I asked.

'Uh-huh! Thought you had fallen asleep.'

'No,' I said, 'I was resting.'

'You must be starving. Before we eat—I've brought a present for you.'

'For me? No no! I don't want any present, no one has ever given me a present.'

'Here it is. Here they are. Feel them. It's one but it's two. It's a pair of dark glasses. Put them on. I want to have my lunch with one of the prettiest girls in the world.' He handed me a pair of glasses. I put them on.

'You are—beautiful. Not pretty. Beautiful.'

'I love them,' I said. 'Are you wearing your dark glasses, Gordon?'

'I am not,' he said. 'I want to look at you.'

'Really beautiful!' I said in unbelief. How could I believe him?

'You will look even more beautiful to me after I have eaten my chow.'

We sat against the tree. We ate Spring-rolls. We drank beautiful fruity stuff from bottles. Not coke. Ole Pa and Rose-ann drink coke.

'Gordon,' I asked. 'What is this wonderful drink?'

'Wonderful? It's pineapple juice. You like it?' He sounded sleepy.

'Yes,' I said, 'I like it.' I felt sleepy myself. It was very warm. I leant back against the tree again.

When I woke up it was much cooler. Much quieter. I knew that I was by myself, that it was night. I always know when night has come. Everything sounds different. Small sounds become louder at night. I was scared.

'Gordon?' I said. I knew he was not there. Had he ever been with me? I felt about for my bead box. He had been with me. When had he gone? Why hadn't he woken me up? Would I ever see him again? Would I die if I never saw him again? My one, apart from Scum-dorg, apart from Mr Faber, my one friend. Yes, I would at least want to die.

I folded my arms about my knees. Made myself as small as I could. I had told Ole Pa I would not mind how late he came for me. What time was it?

I listened for ever and ever and I heard the far-away clock strike nine times. Would he never come?

Was the night black? Could anyone see me? I hoped for the first time in my life that the night was black because another wise saying of Ole Pa's had come true.

Due, I suppose to all the pineapple juice I had greedily drunk, I had by all means to—you know what! It had suddenly become a matter beyond me. It was not whether I wanted; it had to come out.

'Excuse me! Is anyone here?' I asked in a small voice. 'Anyone here?' I asked much louder . . .

I felt much better. I sat and thought over every wonderful, every grand moment of the day.

I was sorry to hear Ole Pa's voice calling me.

CHAPTER SIX

I would have liked to stay under my tree in the park all night.

I knew by his voice that Ole Pa was more than a little stinking. Ole Pa was so stinking that it was a miracle we ever made it back to the room.

Rose-ann had not come in. I was glad about that.

Ole Pa flopped on to his bed and began to snore. I removed his top denture and put it in a glass of water.

Once his denture had gone part way down his throat. Ole Pa had nearly passed out that time.

I worked, neatening up the room, washed out Rose-ann's nylons and undies. I cleaned Ole Pa's shoes, made up Rose-ann's bed—did everything that should've been done during the day.

I crawled into my own bed. I was but tired. I wanted to lie straight and still, get the stiffness out of my legs, let my mind go back over the day.

As soon as I lay down all the worries in the world hit me.

What would happen when Rose-ann and Ole Pa saw the beads all strung? They were smart. They would know for sure that I hadn't done them all myself. What would I do?

Mr Faber was calling tomorrow. Then I could not go to Park. I was calling park, park, not *the* park. Like it was Heaven. No one said *the* Heaven.

What was I to do? Perhaps Mr Faber would take me to Park? He might! Mr Faber himself always said I should get out in 'bark.' 'Oh, Mr Faber,' I prayed, 'take me to Park tomorrow.' No no! Mr Faber was not the one to pray to. I knew better'n that.

'Dear Holy Father in Heaven,' I prayed. 'Let Mr Faber take me to Park tomorrow. Let Gordon be there. Let me have at least one more happy day. I don't expect many happy days. Give me at least one more. Thank you for my blessings, Lord. Amen. S-e-l-i-n-a. Selina praying here, Lord.'

The best thing I ever learnt from the radio is that there is a God. Not a God, but God in Heaven.

If I hadn't learnt this from the radio I would've thought that God and Jesus Christ were dirty words.

Sometimes, from habit and copying those around me, I misuse those Names. I'm sorry about that.

I would love to go into a church.

I can never listen to Sunday church. Rose-ann hates to hear anything about God. Ole Pa gets hopping mad if I dial into church. 'It's all a lot of up your arse.' That's what Ole Pa and Rose-ann are like about God.

I listen to other day church, though. I listened to Billy Graham a few years back. Man! From him I heard that Jesus Christ died for and loves me. I was flattened. I couldn't believe it.

It's true though!

After my prayer I stopped worrying and fell asleep.

CHAPTER SEVEN

'Hoo Hoo! Me and my sun-glasses. Get a load of lover-girl in her sun-glasses.' Rose-ann woke me up, poking at my shoulder.

I sat up. 'What did you say, Rose-ann?' I asked. I felt full of sleep. Rose-ann I could tell had been out on the town. The room reeked with the smell of liquor. Rose-ann only drinks liquor when she goes out on the town. She must have a new friend.

So did I. So did I have a new friend. I was wide, but wide awake.

'What did you say, Rose-ann?' I asked again.

'I said, dumb-bell, I said I got me a fine new pair of sun-glasses,' said Rose-ann.

Jesus! My present! I'd left my present on the bureau. How was I ever to get them back from Rose-ann, who, as Ole Pa said, was a hard one to say the least. I must be smart.

'Are those sun-glasses the sun-glasses that were on the bureau?' I asked.

'Sure are. Sure and certain are.'

'Rose-ann. They belong to someone else.'

'Not teny more they tont,' said Rose-ann. How her words tripped and splashed against each other. I must stop noticing. I must concentrate on getting my glasses back. My present, my present from Gordon.

'I found them in the park yesterday. I'm going to see if the person who dropped 'em comes and looks for them today.'

'Says you.' Rose-ann went to the bathroom and I heard her gargling.

'Shut up in there. Do you have to behave like a pig?' Ole Pa was in a bad mood. He kept on bawling until Rose-ann quit her gargle. Noise also put Rose-ann in a mood. I could tell she was mad. She turned the water on full.

'You there, fat bottom,' she yelled at me. 'Out of bed. Up an' at it girl.'

I got out of bed. I wondered where she had put my present. I had no way of knowing.

'So you had a day in the park?' asked Rose-ann high tone. 'How was your day in the park? Was it like—Wow! Well, was it?'

'It was exactly like—Wow!' I said. Could this be me—me speaking to Rose-ann? So grown-up, so cool.

'You sick or something?' asked Rose-ann. She came up close to me.

'I never felt finer,' I answered. In my new voice 'n manner.

'How you feel now—huh?' I was so surprised at my new manner that I forgot to duck. 'Feel like—Wow!—now?' she asked.

I did not feel like—Wow! I sure had a sore face.

'I washed your nylons, Rose-ann. I cleaned up. Everything in the room is fine. You can see that, can't you, Rose-ann.'

'You had better,' said Rose-ann. 'How did you go with the beads?'

'I did quite a few,' I said. I just hoped she would not look at the beads. I could never explain.

'How many is that?' Ole Pa was scratching his stomach. He scratched so loud I was always feared he would scratch into himself. 'What time did I pick you up last night, Sleena? How many beads you do? Uh-hu-hoo-hoo-haaaa!' Ole Pa yawned with the whole of his body. I didn't like it, but Rose-ann, it made her desperate. She lit into him. I was sure glad that she did.

I switched on the radio.

Frank Sinatra was singing—'All the waay . . .' I began to

whistle. I wish I could hear a recording of my whistling. I know it is the best thing I do. I make grand ups and downs. I whistle fine, for sure.

'Hush up! Hush your mouth. Get the coffee going.' Ole Pa had a hang-over, but bad. He went into the tiny bathroom and began to shave.

After he had shaved he would be nicer. He always was. Man! I was glad I never had to shave. What a bloody mess I would make of myself, if I shaved. I was suddenly glad I was a girl. I'd never even thought such a thing before.

'Bu-ut, if I'm going to love you . . .' sang Frank Sinatra.

'Jumping Jehoshaphat! Who done all these beads?' yelled Rose-ann.

Ah-ah! Here, I thought, comes trouble. 'What gives with all the beads graded and strung?' asked Rose-ann.

'I done them,' I said. 'I did them,' I corrected myself. 'Who else? Who else ever does beads, but me?'

'You asking for another slap on the puss? You offering the other cheek?' asked Rose-ann. 'No one person could do all them beads in one day. Come clean. Something stinks about these beads.' She waited for my answer.

It is hard for me not to tell the truth. There have been so few times, so few things that would make me lie. The few times, when I was small I had said 'No—Sleena didn't do it,' when, truth to tell, Sleena had, Ole Pa had paddled the daylights out of me with his belt. I usually came out with the truth, no matter what.

'Well?' asked Rose-ann. 'Ole Pa,' she yelled. 'Take a gander at the beads Sleena says she done. You reckon Sleena done these beads?'

'Yesterday?' asked Ole Pa. 'Done all those beads yesterday? Impossible.' Ole Pa was waiting too.

'Sleena?' asked Rose-ann.

'If I didn't do them, who did?' I asked. 'The beads are done. Ready for Mr Faber. I told you if you let me go to the park I could work double. I know I can do better work out there in the clean air. What are you flipping your lids for? The beads are done aren't they?'

'It's curious, that's all,' said Rose-ann slowly. 'I don't, as you say, know why we are flipping our lids. It just don't seem possible. I don't like things that ain't possible, that's all.'

'Me too,' said Ole Pa. 'You done all that work in one day?' He scratched his head. 'You got me scratching my head.'

'Ole Pa,' I said. 'You didn't pick me up till mighty late last night. I just went on working. That's all.'

'In the dark?' asked Ole Pa. All these years Ole Pa had lived in the same room with a blind girl. He can never realise that dark and light don't exist for the blind—only dark.

'Yes, Ole Pa. In the dark!' I said.

'It's wonderful. In the dark!' said Ole Pa again.

'Tell Faber to bring you more work,' said Rose-ann. 'I've known you was holding out on us. When I think of the way you have bludged, when I think of the lousy few dozen strings of beads you been turning out all these years, I sure could sock you one, Sleena D'arcey—but good.'

'Lay off Sleena,' said Ole Pa.

'Sleena's my kid. I'll say what I like to her.'

'You—you slut. You know-all, know-nuttin, you no-good. You are my kid. I'll say what I like to you. Lay off Sleena. Tell Faber to bring the usual amount of work, Sleena.' Ole Pa went back to his shaving.

'Hoo hoo!' yelled Rose-ann. 'Wash yourself good you need a good wash, for sure. You stink. Pooh! But you sure stink. Pooh!'

Ole Pa came out again, I knew he would. As Rose-ann knew he would. Off they went in a crazy blow . . .

They couldn't help it. It was always the way. Rose-ann said Faber was to bring me more work. That I was not to go to the park.

Ole Pa said just opposite.

I meant to go anyway.

I made the coffee. Rose-ann and Ole Pa could never face up to more than coffee in the morning. Me, I was always hungry for breakfast, but waited until they had left the room. Times are, I've felt dizzy, longing for food.

This morning I was only dizzy with longing for them to get on their ways.

Would they never hush up!

Rose-ann acted like the rats were after her. She gulped down her coffee. Said it was 'slush . . . hog-wash . . .' I smelt her putting on her face.

She left for 'Ladies' yelling that she—Rose-ann—would have a thing or two, or even three, to say when she came home if I, Sleena, had been taken to the park.

'I'm warning you,' yelled Rose-ann, and she banged the door shut.

Ole Pa opened it and yelled after her: 'Up yours!—you no count, three-bucks-a-time broad.'

Rose-ann came running back and screamed, 'Take that damning remark back. Change that three to ten. Say ten bucks, you dirty, dirty bum.'

They had another blow.

Time was running out on them. They had to punch a clock every morning. I've always wondered why. I must ask someone. Gordon.

I picked up the glass Ole Pa's denture was swimming in.

'Ole Pa,' I said.

'Shut up,' said Ole Pa.

'Here's your denture, Ole Pa,' I said.

'I know that better'n you. I got eyes to see.'

Ole Pa was in a dirty mood for sure. He was an old man. Old people should have a quiet time. If Ole Pa and I lived alone, lived without Rose-ann, I know he would have a quiet time like old people should. He would not have to get shut of me because I am quiet myself. Instead of getting drunk every night I lay odds that he would stay to home at times and play dominoes. Maybe I'm wrong. But no harm in laying odds.

'Ole Pa,' I said again. 'Mr Faber is taking me to Park today (Man! I didn't know if he was or not. Some liar I was . . .) don't mind how late you pick me up, Ole Pa. Just so long as you do.'

Ole Pa took his denture to the bathroom to clean. I followed him. 'Any time, any ole time'll do, Ole Pa. I don't mind how late.'

The denture was in place. 'Tsk-tsh-tsuu . . . You heard what I said to your Ma? You heard what I said to Rose-ann?'

'I heard you, Ole Pa.'

'Well!' said Ole Pa. 'Same to you.' He banged the door so hard—me, and everything in the room that wasn't nailed or glued down, jumped.

The room was mine. I turned off the radio and stood in the middle of the room and listened to the quiet.

I had my bath. Ate my breakfast. Neatened up, and washed out yesterday's clothes. I used a brush on the collar of Ole Pa's shirt, the inside part. I did the same to the collar of my blouse.

I had so few clothes. Only things that Rose-ann had finished with. I'd never had a new dress of my own. Why,

after all should I? How senseless to spend hard-earned
money on clothes for a girl who couldn't see them, who no
one ever saw. I have a bit of sense. I agreed that this was
right and good. But today I wanted to look real neat.

No use to try on Rose-ann's new clothes. She had moved
into two sizes bigger than of yore. I would stay dressed in
my wrapper until Mr Faber came. I would ask Mr Faber
which of my clothes looked most fitting for a day in the
park.

I sat waiting. The beads were finished in the box. There
was work I could've done in the room. I didn't want to
work. How late Mr Faber was. Had Mr Faber ever not
come? I thought back. No. He had always come.

He would come. I would have to wait.

Now the room was too quiet. I turned on the radio.

'Are you suwah, suwah, that your breath is sweet? To
make suwah, take a . . .' I changed the station.

'. . . to the stars . . .' sang Mr Como. I listened to Mr
Como sing through his song. I thought how fine it must be to
be the way he was. At the top of his profession! Very nice.

Well, I wasn't doing so badly. Here I was. Soon Mr Faber,
and maybe Scum-dorg, would come. Soon, maybe, I would
be on my way to Park. There maybe . . .

Scum-dorg scratched on the door. I had been so lost in my
thoughts that I'd not heard Mr Faber coming upstairs and
along the hall.

(It took Rose-ann twelve steps to come along the hall. Old
Pa took seven long steps, Mr Faber eight.)

I opened the door. Scum-dorg rubbed his nice rough head
against my wrapper. I bent down and held his rough head in
my hands.

'Hullo, hullo best dog in the world,' I said.

'Huhhuhhuh . . . huhhuhhuh,' said Scum-dorg.

'Good mornink!' said Mr Faber.

CHAPTER EIGHT

I leant back against the trunk of my dearly loved oak tree.

'Don't weep, don't cry, Selina,' I told myself.

'You did have a happy day. Some folks don't even have one happy day to remember.'

I began to cry. I cried very softly.

I don't need a handkerchief when I cry, because I cry no tears. I only need a handkerchief when I have a cold.

Mr Faber had been glad to bring me here to the park. He had been, he told me, 'more than glat.'

Mr Faber had told me to wear my blue cotton blouse, the one with white spots on it.

Before we had left the room, with a desperate hope I'd asked Mr Faber to look around and see if he could locate my sun-glasses. He had found them.

I'd put them on. 'How do I look, Mr Faber?'

'Wah! You look—luffly, shust—luffly."

He had helped me lay out my rug. Arranged my bead boxes.

Scum-dorg had known it was a special thing, this coming to Park. He snuffed and rolled on the grass for the joy of it. Mr Faber had given a running description of Scum-dorg's behaviour.

'On his tum-ack, now on his barkbone . . . on his tumack again . . . O—fah he rools . . .'

We had laughed at Scum-dorg, and Scum-dorg had gone real crazy.

I had been too happy. That's dangerous. One should never be too happy.

Now I was crying because Mr Faber had left me just as the far-away clock struck the hour of nine. It had struck again and again.

It was midday. I was alone.

Gordon had not come. He was not coming. Why had I thought he would?

I knew as sure as I was blind that he was not coming and I blamed only myself for thinking that he would come.

Whatever had given me the idea that he would bother to
see me again?

'I come here every day,' he had said. Well! So what? It
was a big park. A very big park.

I had worked like crazy doing beads for the first hour.
Slacked off on the second. Done only two strings during the
last.

I had better get on with my beads. I sat up straight and
began to whistle. I whistled my best. I whistled:

> When Irish eyes are smiling . . .
> All the world seems bright an' gay . . .

I thought I'd never heard my whistling so good, I couldn't
believe my whistling could sound so good. I realised that
someone else was whistling with me. Clear, sweet and strong.
I stopped.

'Don't stop, Selina,' said Gordon. He sat down beside me. I
heard him begin to grade the beads.

I couldn't go on whistling. How could I? My throat felt
strange. My heart beat with tiny, hasty little taps.

'Hullo, Gordon,' I said.

'Hi! Hi there, beautiful!' said Gordon.

CHAPTER NINE

Crying one minute. Laughing the next. That was me. Gordon made me work so fast. I had never worked so fast. No
sooner was one thread full, another was in my hand.

'You don't know the first thing about threading beads,' said
Gordon. 'If I had been threading beads all the years you say
you have been threading beads, I would put you to shame.'
That's what he said. But I knew he meant:

'You're cute and clever. I like you. I like sitting in the park
under an oak tree with you. I like helping you to thread
beads. I think you are one of the prettiest girls (with sun-
glasses on) in the world. I like you, Selina D'arcey, for sure.
I don't know how I was so sure of this, but just as sure and in

the same way as I know there's a God above, I knew it. So I laughed.

'Gordon,' I said. 'We mustn't do too many beads.'

'I thought you were paid for doing them?'

'Well I am. Of course Mr Faber pays . . .'

'So?' asked Gordon.

'If I get too many done with you helping me—when you're not helping me and I don't get so many done—I will get trouble for not doing so many as I do when you *are* helping me,' I told him.

'I beg your pardon,' said Gordon. 'Were you speaking to me?'

'Yes,' I said.

'May I ask when you last visited the land of Gibble-Gabble? It has been quite a time since *I* was last there, I have forgotten the language. Will you translate for me please?' His voice was so serious. When he spoke seriously like that I could imagine that Gordon's face was laughing. I laughed at him.

'No. No, *sir*,' I told him. 'You'll just have to brush up on your foreign languages when you are with me.'

'Hai, hai! kasakumari—masu', said Gordon.

'What?' I asked in astonishment.

'You should not say "What?" like that. You should say, "I beg your pardon?" I was brushing up on one of my many foreign languages. I said, "Yes, yes, I shall do as you say" in Japanese.'

'You speak Japanese?' I was deeply amazed.

'No,' said Gordon, 'I know a few phrases. I know a bit of Japanese. A bit of French—lousy French—I mean, *my* French is lousy. A bit of German, and so on.'

'You are very smart,' I said proudly. I felt very proud having a friend who could speak a bit of so many languages.

'No, I'm not smart. You, with your Gibble-Gabble, are the smart one.'

'Me? Smart?'

'You!' said Gordon.

'Oh, no . . .' I began.

'You dare to disagree with me? Who are you to say my friend Selina D'arcey is not smart. I challenge you. I insist that you say Selina is smart. Let me hear you.'

I began to laugh. I bet no one ever laughed so much as I did that day, that second day in Park with Gordon.

'Do not laugh. Simply say, "Selina—is smart."'

'Selina,' I laughed, 'is smart.'

'Thank you,' said Gordon. 'I can't stand people knocking my friends.'

'Me too,' I said. 'If anyone knocks Mr Faber or Scum-dorg or you, just God help them that's all.' My voice was very deep.

'Why are we the favoured few?'

'Because,' I told him, 'you and Scum-dorg and Mr Faber ate the best and only friends I have in the world.'

'You are kidding?'

'No.'

'Then, until yesterday, Mr Faber and his dog with the unfortunate name—Scum-dorg—were your only friends?'

'Yes,' I said.

I held out my hand to take the next beads from Gordon. They were not ready. I knew he was still sitting there. Was he angry with me?

'Gordon?' I asked.

'Yes?'

'Why are you so quiet?'

'I'm,' Gordon cleared his throat. I sure hoped sitting on the grass had not given him a cold. 'I'm thinking it's about time we had our lunch,' said Gordon.

'Lunch! I wish I'd brought lunch for you. Excuse me for not bringing it. Are you coming down with a cold?' I asked.

'Cold? Oh! No, I never come down with colds. And don't you ever bring lunch for me. I am the bringer of lunches. Surely you know that. Today I made these salad and chicken sandwiches. I hope they meet with Madam's approval. I also brought Madam's favourite drink—to wit—pineapple juice.'

I'd never tasted anything as good as the sandwiches.

'You really made them?' I asked.

'You doubt me?' Gordon asked sadly.

'A little.'

'You are right to doubt me. I admit to buying them. Do you want a drink now, Selina?'

I longed for a drink. Remembering—you know what! I said:

'No thank you, Gordon, I do not care to drink today.'

'Not drink! Not drink today? You went for this drink in such a big way. Why don't you like it today? Shall I go, shall I get a coke for you?'

No one, not even Mr Faber had ever, I'm sure, cared whether I drank at all, let alone *what* I cared to drink. It was fabulous. I would wake up. I stuck my nail into my hand. It hurt. I was not dreaming.

'No coke, thank you, Gordon.'

Gordon was quiet again. 'Selina, you don't have to worry about anything. I don't know why we humans consider ourselves so much higher than dogs or pussy cats, even higher than birds or bees. Honey! Just about forty steps from here there is a "place for little girls" to wash their hands, etc. etc. I will take you those forty steps any time you say the word. Will you have a drink now, Selina? asked Gordon.

'I vould luff a drink,' I said in my Mr Faber voice. I drank two bottles straight off. How had I ever lived so long without having a friend?

'You think then we have done as many beads as we dare?' asked Gordon.

'Yes, for sure.'

'What shall we do then until five o'clock?'

'Do you have to go at five o'clock?'

'I do. If you expect to lead a life of luxury—swilling down pineapple juice—I have to leave at five o'clock.'

'What time is it now?' I asked. I had not noticed the far-away clock chime even once.

'It is now three twenty-five,' said Gordon. Only ninety-five minutes left! Would he come tomorrow? I had to know.

'Will you—do you think you will step this way tomorrow, Gordon?' I asked. I held my breath.

'I was going to ask you that. Tomorrow is Sunday. Do you come here on Sunday?'

Jesus! Sunday! I had no more chance of coming to Park on Sunday than I had of walking alone those forty steps to the place where girls washed their hands.

'Will you come on Monday?' I asked in a little voice.

'I shall be here sharp at noon on Monday,' said Gordon.

'I'm glad,' I said. We sat quiet for a long time. I had never been so happy in all my life.

'Do you like poetry, Selina?' asked Gordon. His voice sounded far away.

'Poetry! of course.' I knew only a little poetry. You don't hear much poetry on the radio.

'Do you like this?' In the same far-off voice Gordon said:

> 'Across the foaming river
> The old bridge bends its bow;
> My father's fathers built it
> In ages long ago.
>
> They never left the farmstead
> Past which the waters curled.
> Why should one ever wander—
> When here is all the world?'

The far-away clock chimed four times. It hurt me.
'Will you say some more poetry, please, Gordon?' I asked.
'You say some for me.'
'I only know songs. I really only know songs.'
'Say me a little song,' said Gordon.
I suddenly felt shy. I'd never felt so shy before in my life.
'What kind of song?' I asked.
'The first little old song you think of.'
No, no, I couldn't do that. I thought of all the silliest songs.
The only songs I could think of were ridiculous.
'I can't,' I said.
'Then I shall say an old Chinese poem for you.'
I was glad that he didn't ask me again. I waited to hear the
old Chinese poem.

> 'On the river island—
> The ospreys are echoing us
> Where is the pure-hearted girl
> To be our princess?
>
> Long lotus, short lotus,
> Leaning with the current,
> Turns like our prince in his quest
> For the pure-hearted girl.
>
> He has sought and not found her.
> Awake, he has thought of her,
> Asleep, he has dreamed of her,
> Dreamed and tossed in his sleep.
>
> Long lotus, short lotus.
> Pluck it to left and to right,

Make ready with lutes and with harps
For the pure-hearted girl.

Long lotus, short lotus,
Cook it for a welcome,
Be ready with bells and with drums
For the pure-hearted girl.'

'Do you like that old, old Chinese poem, Selina?' asked
Gordon.

'Yes,' I said. 'I like it.'

'So do I,' said Gordon. 'Selina, let's take a walk.'

'A walk?'

'There's a garden of summer roses a short way over the
grass. Red roses. Will you come?'

I thought: I'll do what ever you say. Just tell me what to
do and I'll do it. I said: 'Yes I would like to take a walk.'

The scent of the red roses was as sweet as knowing Gordon. As sweet as being out in the world with a friend by my
side. I knew I would never forget the scent of the summer
roses in the park.

Gordon had scooped up a handful of fallen petals. I held
them in my hand. I kept them in my closed hand. I had
never held anything so nice.

Two people had come while we had been away. They
were sitting a way off on the bench Gordon had sat on until
he began to sit on the grass with me. They soon moved off. I
was glad when they did. We hadn't spoken a word while the
strangers had been near us.

'Gordon,' I said.

'Ummm?'

'Before I met you,' I said, 'I thought the best word in the
world was "bright." I've always loved the word "bright." I
suppose I like the word so much because I know it is
different from "dark" . . .'

'And now?' asked Gordon.

'And now, since I know you, I know that "friend" is the
grandest, biggest and best word . . .'

'I know a better word.'

I was rather down about this. Then I realised that he must
have many friends—about six friends perhaps. The idea of
having six friends was too much to think of.

'What is a better word?'

Gordon lit one of his cigarettes. I liked the smell of the tobacco. It crept towards me, I took a quick sniff as it passed by me.

'Is your favourite word a secret?' I asked.

'A secret? Lord, no! "Tolerance." '

' "Tolerance"! I don't think much of that to have for a favourite word.' I was disappointed.

'Don't you?' Gordon asked.

' "Friend" is much nicer, much warmer,' I insisted.

'Without tolerance there can be no friendship.'

I'd never thought of that. I'd always thought "to tolerate" meant "to put up with it." When I had a bad toothache, Rose-ann had told me, 'You'll just have to tolerate it.' I couldn't. I'd worked the tooth back and forth, back and forth. The pain of doing that added to the pain of the tooth —bad, for sure. After two days, the tooth had come out.

'I don't like the word. "Friend" is so much better,' I said in my deep voice.

Gordon laughed and said: 'Then opinion is divided.' He seemed not to care much. I cared. I wanted to have the same word as he did.

'Why is it such a good word?' I asked.

'Among many things,' said Gordon, 'it means freedom of thought. It does away with bigotry. If you have it, it means you have a broad mind. It means: don't knock your brother —your neighbour—don't knock *anyone* because he is different, looks, thinks, eats, loves, worships or hates differently from the way you do all those things yourself.'

How '*bout* that! Man! he had a fine word, for sure.

'And you?' I asked Gordon if he was tolerant. I knew that he was, but I knew that it was nearly five o'clock. I hoped that if I kept him talking he might stay a while.

'And me?'

'Full of tolerance?'

'No,' said Gordon. 'I'm intolerant of folks' intolerance. I wear dark glasses to hide the anger of my hideous intolerance. I, Selina—friend Selina—am not tolerant. Tolerance is beyond me.'

How 'bout *that*. I'd have laid big odds he was full of tolerance.

The far-away clock sounded. Five times it sounded. Dong-a dong-a dong-a dong-a dong-a . . .

'Thank you for my lovely day, Gordon,' I said.

'The day was lovely because you, Selina, were in the park. Because you allowed me to share it with you.'

'No, oh no . . .'

'Yes,' said Gordon. 'Make no mistake about it.'

'You will come on Monday?' I asked. I had to hear him say he would once more.

'For sure,' mocked Gordon.

'That's good,' I said.

A grand thing happened a short time after Gordon had gone to work at his newspaper. A fine warm thing took place.

Scum-dorg ran snuffling over the grass towards me. I of course didn't know it was Scum-dorg until I felt his nice rough head poke against my knee.

I could've cried for happiness. 'Scum-dorg, best dog in the world!' I cried out.

'Good evenink, Sleena!' said Mr Faber. 'Me ant Scum-dorg —ve vas shust taking a valk in bark. Vould you like it if ve valk you to home, Sleena?'

Would I like it? Would I like it!

'Oh, Mr Faber,' I cried. 'How tolerant you are, you are full of tolerance. You are a fine tolerant friend . . .'

'Nah! shust valking, shust valking in bark. Come, Sleena. Ve walk you to home . . .'

CHAPTER TEN

For the first time since for ever Ole Pa came home direct from 'Mens.' Came home with, as he said, 'nary a beer in his empty belly.'

If he'd come home just ten minutes before I would not've been in the room.

He came home, he said, because he'd had it back of his mind to take me to the park for a walk. He'd been thinking about me being cooped up times an' for ever and he'd been sorry he'd not taken me in the morning.

'Would you like to go to the park now, Sleena?' I couldn't answer him. I just couldn't. This day's happenings were a bit too much to be understood. Could I take all this happiness, this pampering, could I take it in my stride? I felt a bit scared.

'What's up, Sleena?' asked Ole Pa.

I took a deep breath. 'Nothing is up, Ole Pa. I just feel glad that you thought of me, that's all.'

'What you wearing Rose-ann's sun-glasses for?' asked Ole Pa.

I took off my glasses. 'Just for fun,' I said.

'She'll use a hot tongue on you if she sees you. You want I should take you to the park?' Ole Pa was getting raspy. I must be tolerant.

'Ole Pa,' I said. 'Don't take me to the park tonight. I know you are longing to go out and get shikkered. So you can go out now! Will you take me on Monday—in the morning—instead? Will you, Ole Pa?'

'Maybe,' said Ole Pa. He took a bath and changed into a fresh shirt. 'I feel pretty good, Sleena.' That's what he said.

So did I. I had the laugh on Rose-ann and Ole Pa first time in my life. I had made plans with Ole Pa for going to Park, Monday. Only one thing was bad! Sunday came before Monday. Sunday was the worst day of the week always.

The reason Sunday is such a bad day always, is because Sadie comes to visit with Rose-ann. Sadie is Rose-ann's friend.

I hate Sadie.

Ole Pa lights out as soon as she arrives. If he would stay things wouldn't be so bad for me, maybe.

Ole Pa hates Sadie too. 'You here again? You big fat slob.' That's the way he says hullo to Sadie every Sunday morning.

'Yeah,' says Sadie. 'An' from one big fat *slob* to another, how come youse still not in the nut house? How come a diseased old poodle like you hasn't been picked up by the dog catcher?'

Sadie is much smarter than Ole Pa when it comes to being rude, although Ole Pa himself is no slouch. He never answers her. Just lights out. At this time, only at these times, I wish I was Ole Pa. I have to stay in the room—all day—every Sunday with Rose-ann and Sadie.

This Sunday I made up my mind things were going to be

mighty different. I knew that Sadie and Rose-ann would not
be different. It would be me—Selina.

Sadie was Rose-ann's friend. It was up to me to have
tolerance. It could just be that Rose-ann and Sadie might not
care for *my* friends. For Gordon and Mr Faber—I knew
without doubt that they would certainly not care for Scum-
dorg. I would be tolerant if it killed me.

'Hi! Hi, Rose-ann doll,' said Sadie. 'How's a gal—huh?'

'Take the load offa your feet, doll,' said Rose-ann. 'I'm
fine, Sadie. How's things?'

'Lousy, but no good—lousy,' said Sadie.

'How come?' asked Rose-ann.

Sadie told Rose-ann just why things were so lousy. I listened and realised that indeed with Sadie things were lousy.

When Sadie had been young, she had been 'a dish.' She had
been a call-girl of high repute. She was always telling Rose-
ann how very high her repute had been. It was hard for
Sadie to take in that she had gone off, had these days, a hard
time to earn a bare living even.

I felt my tolerance beginning to work. Poor, fat Sadie, I
thought. I felt, for the first time, sorry for Sadie.

'Hullo, Sadie,' I said.

Sadie gave a loud scream. 'Man!' She pretended to be very
frightened. 'Man! Dig that crazy ghost! Did you hear a crazy
ghost tellin' me hullo, did you, Rose-ann?'

'Hoo hoo! No, I never heard no ghost, I heard nothing,'
said Rose-ann.

This happened every Sunday. Sadie says, because of me
being blind and not seeing her, she, Sadie, can't see me.
When I make the lunch and supper, if I put a clean glass on
the table for Sadie, she screams: 'Dig that cer-azy ghost
again!'

This Sunday I said in my deep voice, 'Don't be upset,
Sadie. It's no ghost. It's me, Selina.'

'You standing for her giving cheek to me, Rose-ann?'
asked Sadie.

'I am not,' said Rose-ann. 'Tuck your tongue in, Sleena.
Bring me and Sadie coffee.'

'With pleasure,' I said.

'My God!' said Sadie, 'you taking that lip from *that?*'

'I am not,' said Rose-ann. 'If I wasn't so tired, Sleena, if I
wasn't too doggone tired, I'd get up an' sock you.'

'Let me,' said Sadie. Sadie must have put out her foot very suddenly. I fell flat.

'Dig that,' she said.

'Hoo hoo hoo, Sadie, you slay me,' said Rose-ann.

My tolerance was worn to a thread. I didn't try any more. I did everything for Rose-ann and her friend that I was told to. I did the best I could. Sadie and Rose-ann had never ridden me so hard. It didn't matter.

> 'Long lotus—short lotus . . .
> Be ready with bells and with drums . . .'

I said as much as I could remember of Gordon's poem. Said it under my breath. Said it over and over.

Rose-ann and Sadie never drew a quiet breath all day. If one wasn't talking, the other was. Sometimes they both talked at the same time. When this happened they talked louder and louder, each one determined to win out. Sadie won out every time. She has a very strong character. So, of course, does Rose-ann. I'm not knocking Rose-ann.

Neither Rose-ann nor Sadie ever works on Sunday. Sometimes they have said what a waste the small room down the hall was—never used on Sunday. They liked to really take it easy. Talk and laugh and eat and drink on Sunday.

Sadie always brought a bottle of Bourbon. She drank it, every drop, every Sunday, all to herself. Rose-ann drank only Coke—on Sundays, that is.

'Clears my system off for the week,' she says.

The bourbon always made Sadie hilarious.

'Look-a me Dad! Look-a Sadie—hilarious—I'm hi-lar-ri-us! Woo woo!'

'Sadie, you slay me.' Rose-ann liked Sadie for sure.

Never in all the years Sadie had been coming to the room had they gone out. Sadie would fight her way down the steps, late at night, when she had emptied her bottle. Rose-ann always stood and watched her.

' 'Bye, Sadie,' she would yell.

' 'Bye, Rose-ann doll.'

' 'Bye, Sadie . . .'

' 'Bye, Rose-ann . . .' Sometimes they would say good-bye at least twenty times, depending how long it took Sadie to negotiate the stairs.

This Sunday, I nearly passed out. I don't know what got into Rose-ann and Sadie. About nine o'clock, for no reason whatsoever, right out of the blue, unbelievably, Rose-ann said: 'How 'bout we—you'n I—take in a movie, Sadie?'

'What the hell for?' asked Sadie.

I was all Sadie's way myself. I'm sure a light touch would've toppled both Sadie and me over with no trouble at all.

'Be a doll,' said Rose-ann. 'Let's take in a movie, Sadie. Huh? Huh?'

'What the hell!' said Sadie. They kept this up for ever. Finally, Rose-ann stuck out her lips. She was sulky. Sadie became the one who had, but just had, to take in a movie.

'Don't be a louse, Rose-ann.'

'I'm not moving from this bed.'

'Don't be a *louse*,' said Sadie.

Let them go. Let them go. Please, God, let them go.

Talk about the power of prayer. Better not knock the power of prayer to me. In five minutes Sadie and Rose-ann had gone out. I knew they wouldn't go to a movie. I knew Rose-ann would stay out all night. I don't know how I knew it but I did, and I was right.

I turned off the radio. The room was beautiful.

> 'Why should one ever wander—
> When here is all the world?'

I said. It sounded fine. I said it again. I cleaned up after Rose-ann and Sadie. I ironed my blue blouse carefully. Tomorrow was Monday. Maybe somewhere in the world was a girl who thought she was luckier, happier than me; that girl was *wrong*. I, S-e-l-i-n-a, Selina, was the happiest.

I took a bath and brushed my 'pale gold hair.' I patted some of Rose-ann's cologne on my 'pale gold skin.' I washed off the cologne. I wanted no part of Rose-ann. I put more cologne on my skin. I would learn tolerance if it slayed me. I lay in my bed. I was happy. I began to cry. I cried and cried, I cried for ever and ever. I just couldn't stop my crying and I did not know why I was crying. I feel asleep.

CHAPTER ELEVEN

When I told Ole Pa that Rose-ann and Sadie had gone out the night before, Ole Pa scratched his head.

'I'm scratching my head,' said Ole Pa.

'Is it a nice day, Ole Pa?' I asked.

'Wouldn't know,' said Ole Pa.

'Please look out the window. Please tell me the sky is blue,' I begged. It just had to be a fine day. It was Monday! Monday.

'Why should you care?' Ole Pa gave a weary old old man's yawn. I felt sad for Ole Pa. He was old and he had to go and work all day at 'Mens.' I was eighteen and I was going to spend a wonderful day in the, in Park, with my dearest friend. With Gordon. What had Ole Pa said?

'I beg your pardon. What did you say, Ole Pa?' He gave an even longer, louder yawn. He spoke as he yawned, I gathered that he had said: 'Why should you care if the day was fine or not!' Why should I care? Had he forgotten his promise to take me to Park? Was he going to be difficult?

With confidence I said a quick prayer. I came a flop with this prayer. Maybe God was weary, like Ole Pa, in a very different way of course, but weary after Sunday. I guess Sunday is a mighty busy day for God. So many people going to church.

'You said you would take me to Park for sure,' I said to Ole Pa.

'When?'

'Today.'

'I mean—when did I say all this?'

'I know you remember, Ole Pa. You will, you are taking me, you are, aren't you?'

'No,' said Ole Pa, 'I ain't.'

He went into the bathroom and began to shave. Better wait till he'd shaved. I should've known better.

Ole Pa sure played 'hard to get.' I did everything I could

(with being unable to see) do for him. I was too eager. It is bad to be too anything, very bad. I forgot to put coffee in the 'perk.' I handed Ole Pa a cup of sugared hot water. Ole Pa never drinks water hot or otherwise, he thinks water is the least!

'You gone mad?' he asked me.

'What's wrong?' I asked.

'Take a noseful of this stuff.'

I smelt. Jesus! I'd forgotten to put in the coffee.

'I'm sorry, Ole Pa, sorry for real. I'll make it again.'

'Getting late. Too late for making it again.'

Late? Was it too late for him to take me to Park? I was dressed and ready. My rug and boxes were packed and ready. Only Ole Pa was stoppping me. I began to cry.

'What's the matter?' asked Ole Pa.

'I want so much to go to Park,' I cried.

'Then what you waiting for?' he asked. 'What you mucking about for? If you want to go to this here wonderful Park, what you messing about for—huh?'

'I can't do this every day you know,' Ole Pa grumbled, as we made our way to the park.

'Of course not! Only sometimes. Just now'n again, huh!' I said.

'Never again. I got more to do with my day than pilot a blind tomato around the city.' He was sure grumpy.

'It's good of you, Ole Pa.'

'Hush up! Here you are. Sit down. Hurry up.'

I didn't sit down. We were, I knew, nowhere near my oak tree.

'Not here, Ole Pa. Where I was before. Near where I was before.' I was trembling with worry. To be in Park! Such a big Park. To be here, and Gordon not to know it.

'Here or nowhere,' said Ole Pa.

'Please, Ole Pa,' I said real quietly.

'Fer Chris' sake!' said Ole Pa, and he took me to my tree.

'I don't mind how late you come, Ole Pa,' I said.

'That's good. Lucky for you, bully for you. What if I don't come—huh? It's on the cards.'

'Good-bye. Thank you, Ole Pa.' I felt the darling trunk of my tree behind my back. The air was sweeter than air had ever been in the world before. I was here. In only four hours . . . in four little hours. Gordon would be here too. Don't cry, Selina, don't cry for happiness, I said. Just a little cry, a little cry for happiness, I begged. All right! Just a little one. I cried—just a little.

CHAPTER TWELVE

Four hours did I say? Four hours—nothing. I hadn't even time to arrange my boxes in front of me. I heard Gordon walking over the grass towards me. Towards me. He was whistling. I joined in.

'Oh what a beautiful mornnn-ning, Oh what a beautiful daaaay . . .' whistled Gordon and Selina.

'Slacker!' said Gordon. He sat down. 'Do you mean to tell me that you have not as yet commenced the day—the beautiful day's quota?'

'Not yet,' I giggled. I don't think I'd ever done that before —giggled, I mean.

'Dis-gray-hase-ful! Shocking! Man! You sure smell sweet today! Did you stay here all night, did you come very early? I think you must have bathed with the flowers this morning. There's a dewy look about you, Miss D'arcey. Tell me, did you bathe with the flowers this morning?'

'No,' I said. 'I used some of Rose-ann's cologne.' Gordon sniffed. 'Very nice. Have you no cologne of your own? Do you have to use Rose-ann's cologne? Tell me.'

'I have one million bottles of cologne,' I said, 'but I, as well as being a slacker, am a thief.'

'No kidding?'

'No kidding.'

'Nice company to be in I'm sure,' said Gordon. 'Hullo, Selina. How are you? You look grand.'

'Grand, I am,' I said.

'You look far too grand to string beads today. You are not a-going to string beads today.'

'No.' There! I'd giggled again.

'I,' said Gordon, 'am going to string beads and you are going to talk to me.'

'Oh no . . .' I began.

'You dare to go against my wishes?'

'Please, Gordon.'

'Please Gordon—what?'

'I always string beads. I've strung for eight years. Every day for eight years. I'd feel queer . . .'

'Do you mean to tell me'—Gordon took a deep breath— 'do you mean to tell me that you have done this piddling work for eight years?' he sounded angry.

'Yes, of course.'

'Selina, don't you read braille? Haven't you been taught any of the wonderful, clever and skilled work that sightless people excel in, in this day and age. Tell me?' I felt ashamed. I sure felt sad and ashamed.

'I've been taught nothing,' I said.

'It hardly seems possible.'

'I don't mind,' I said.

'Hardly possible. Selina, you need a promoter.'

'Do I, Gordon?'

'For sure,' said Gordon.

'I'd like a promoter,' I said.

While we had been talking he had been busy with the beads. I could hear him working. At first it was hard for me to sit doing nothing. I kept wringing my hands together.

'Here,' said Gordon, 'play with this.' I took a hard object from him. Hard and square.

'What is it?' I asked.

'Open it. Just open the lid,' said Gordon.

'It is a wooden box,' I said.

'Yes.'

I fumbled a little. My finger touched a metal knob. The lid flew back and music, clear and fairy sweet floated from the box in my hands. The music was new to me and yet I knew it was very old. I could tell by the tinkling music that it was a little weary, almost too weary to play again. How long I wondered had it been kept prisoner in the little square box that had an old smell. A sad, tender little smell. How long?

'Il pleut, il pleut, bergère,' Gordon sang in the deepest softest voice.

The music hesitated a moment. Was it going to stop? I hoped it wouldn't stop. I imagined an old sweet lady, I'd never known an old sweet lady, but I imagined one. She seemed to be too tired to take another step! She was sweet and brave . . . The music went on and finished. I closed the lid. I'd never been so sad and happy. I could never bear to open the lid and make the sad, tired song work again. I loved and wanted to care for it.

'Is it a music-box, Gordon?' I asked.

'Yes.'

'Does it belong to you?' I asked.

'No.' He was silent, then he said: 'It belongs to you, Selina.'

He was giving me another present. This I would never take back to the room. I thought of Rose-ann, Sadie.

'Thank you, Gordon,' I said. 'I love it.'

'I thought you would. It was given to one of my ancestors many years ago. Given to her by a man who loved her.'

'Did they get married and live for ever happy?' I asked.

'No,' said Gordon, and I did not like his voice. It was as ugly and bitter as, as a toothache.

'Oh—why not?' I whispered.

'Why not?' Gordon's voice was not like toothache any more. It was like cold water on a cold morning.

'Yes. Why not?'

'It was a long time ago. A long time ago. I've heard—only heard—my mother told me the story. He, the lover of my great great grandmother, he was—from a different world. A world of riches, culture . . .'

'And she?'

Toothache again in Gordon's voice. I knew from experience how bad he felt.

'She was a——' he stopped again. He went on. 'She was just a beautiful woman. Nothing else. She was—*nothing*.' He began to whistle brightly. I wanted to hear more about his great great grandmother.

'Tell me more about her?'

'More! I don't know any more.'

'You must know a little more,' I begged. I held my music-box against my cheek. Rose-ann had often told me I was a nothing. 'You are nothing, but *nothing*,' Rose-ann had said, time and again, ever since I could remember. *She* also had been nothing. Just like me.

'Please!' I asked again.

I heard the click of his lighter and smelt the smell of yet another cigarette.

'He was her lover,' said Gordon.

'Ahh!' I said wisely.

'No,' I said, 'I've a fine memory.'

'You have,' said Gordon. 'You—pure-hearted girl.'

I laughed with happiness. I was a pure-hearted girl. I knew by his voice that that was a fine kind of girl to be.

'I'm letting you down with the beads. You'll be mad with me,' said Gordon.

'I could never be mad with you,' I said, and I laughed again because it was the first time in my life that anyone had said: '*You*'ll be mad with me.' Many times Rose-ann had said: 'I'm mad, but *mad* at you, Sleena.' Sleena? Who was *Sleena*? Not me! I was Selina.

We did the beads together for a while. We worked hard. Gordon was no slouch at doing beads by himself.

Was it O.K., I wondered, for a person to be as happy, plain ordinary happy, as I was? I sure hoped so. Too much of anything is dangerous! I tried not to feel quite so all-fired happy. I felt happier than before.

'What are we having for lunch today, Daddy-o?' I asked in my too happy voice.

'What you feel like, Dad?' Gordon asked me.

'What you bring, Daddy-o?'

'Sliced Polish salami, German potato salad. You like, you dig cold potato salad, sliced Polish salami?'

'Like—Wow!' I said. And Gordon and I laughed together.

By three o'clock enough beads had been done. We had eaten our lunch. I almost cried when we were eating our lunch, but I did not. I almost cried because Gordon said:

'Hold on, Honey! Don't eat that mouthful. A curious little green bug has fallen—ker-plunk—right into your food.' He threw away what I had been going to eat and gave me a fresh, bugless helping. I nearly cried, but I didn't. Too happy, I guess, even to cry from happiness.

'Three o'clock!' said Gordon. He sat down on the grass and asked. 'Under the greenwood tree, Who loves to lie with me, Tuning his merry note unto the sweet bird's throat?'

'I do. Oh I do,' I cried.

We didn't talk very much. I took the opportunity of asking Gordon a few things, only unimportant little things that had always puzzled me, like:

'What exactly is a shadow?' Now I understood *perfectly*. My shadow had always been getting in Rose-ann's way, I thought it part of me. From now on I'd know what shadow was. I asked about ten such things.

After my questions we were silent again. I thought over all the things I'd just learnt. I was glad to be silent.

Then Gordon began to ask me questions. He asked me about Ole Pa, Rose-ann, the room. About Sadie. He listened as though he was really full of interest about everything in my life. I told him everything.

Free as a bird. Free as a bird I asked Gordon if he would take me those forty steps to the place where girls washed their hands, etc. etc. He waited to see no one else was there, so, I suppose, I would not make a fool of myself. I managed with ease. I sure felt fine.

Four o'clock! Only one more hour.

'It's clouding up,' said Gordon. 'What time is Ole Pa coming to pick you up?'

'Clouding up?' I asked.

'Clouding up. There's going to be a summer storm,' said Gordon.

A storm! Jesus! The only thing I was frightened of was a storm. I was terrified of storms. I crawled under my bed when a storm came. How would I be out in a storm?

'How long before the storm comes?' I asked. Try as I did, I could not stop my voice from shaking.

'What's up? Are you afraid of storms?'

'Afraid! Afraid? Who, me?' I asked.

'You?'

'No, of course not,' I said. 'When do you think it will come? I just don't naturally want to be here when it comes. I might get wet, might catch a cold. When's the storm coming?'

'It may not come at all. Even if it does, it won't come till much much later. Fear not, fair lady.'

He asked me again: 'What time is Ole Pa picking you up?'

This I could not answer. Not truthfully. So I said: "Ole Pa leaves "Mens" at six.'

'Six!' said Gordon. 'You'll be O.K. Storm's not due I should say till much later.'

From that time on until the far-away clock donged five times we hardly spoke at all. We sat, and I was, in spite of fear of the coming storm, happy. Although he sat still and quiet, I knew, just like I know about God, that Gordon was happy too.

Gordon packed the bead boxes, wrapped them in the rug and placed them close beside the tree: 'Just in case,' he said, 'the rain comes a little earlier. You should always bring a raincoat, Selina. Bring a raincoat tomorrow.'

Tomorrow! He would, I knew by his voice, be here again tomorrow. No need to ask. He was coming.

'Good-bye, Selina,' said Gordon.

'Good-bye,' I said. 'Parting is such sweet sorrow,' I added in my deep voice.

'Yes,' said Gordon. 'See you tomorrow? You are coming tomorrow?' Gordon, asking me!

He was sorry to go. Sorry to leave me. I heard his steps pass slowly along the path that wasn't very far away, although, Gordon had told me, hidden from sight from under the tree. Gordon walked along the path very slowly. Then— I couldn't hear him any more.

CHAPTER THIRTEEN

I had always thought I'd known what loneliness meant. I hadn't known. I found out for sure when I could no longer hear Gordon's slow footsteps.

Loneliness is worse by far than toothache.

I listened carefully. Very carefully. There was a thing I had to do and I wanted no strange eyes to see me doing it.

I could hear no one. I heard many steps on the path but no soft thuds nearby on the grass.

As close as possible to the trunk of my oak tree I dug a small hole. The earth was hard, it hadn't rained for days, for weeks. It took a long time.

When I put my arm in I knew the hole was about eight inches deep. That was good, that was what I wanted.

I took off my nylon half-slip and hoped for sure that no one was watching.

Wrapping the old wooden box in my slip, the box that had belonged to a beautiful girl who had been—nothing—I put it gently into the hole.

My music-box would be happier here, in this soft quiet grave, than in the room with Rose-ann, drunk Ole Pa. It didn't seem fitting to take it to the room.

'One day, one happy day, I shall take you out again—maybe.' I said this to my music-box, then I put the soil back.

Did I hear the sound of far-away music coming out of the ground? No, I knew I didn't. But I almost thought I heard music.

I sat and waited for Ole Pa.

'Please, God!' I prayed, 'don't let me be caught out in a storm.'

I sat and waited.

Gordon had spoken rightly. I could smell and feel the oncoming storm. The dry earth seemed to be reaching out to the sky; thirsty, like Ole Pa the time he'd hurt his leg and couldn't get out to get shikkered. Rose-ann hadn't brought even one bottle to him.

I could feel the air about me, heavy and dry. Sudden uneasy little whirls of wind came and went. Far away, as far away as for ever, I heard a dull low growl of thunder.

I sat closer to the tree. Even the thought of tomorrow was lost in the terror I knew, sure as I know God, was surely coming to me. To me, here, out in the night, the lonely people-less dark. I stopped praying to God because I knew the storm was coming anyway.

Every thought that came into my mind was uglier than the last. Only last week I had heard a man reading a story over the radio. I heard his voice again saying:

'Wind and rain beat down savagely. Lightning illuminated the dark world, lightning split the sky . . . Between the rolls of thunder . . .' I tried to forget the rest of the story. The storm began, for real.

The wind whirled, the rain beat down savagely. It fell down and the wind blew it under the tree. In seconds, I was drenched. Between the long dreadful rolls of thunder I knew that lightning was illuminating, splitting the sky. I heard it reach out viciously, worse than Sadie. Worse than Rose-ann's friend had reached out for me, that bad night.

I screamed loudly. The noise of the storm was bigger, larger than ever. I couldn't hear my own scream. No one could've heard. I screamed again and again.

'Why am I blind?' I screamed. 'Why can't I *see?* Why can't I get up and run swiftly from this place, this storm?' I screamed for Ole Pa. For Rose-ann. For Mr Faber.

My 'pale gold hair' was plastered to my head, my clothing was part of my wet body. Had a human ever been so wet before? I was human—wasn't I? Wasn't I, Selina, human? I couldn't be.

'*No one ud ever leave a dog go out on a night like this.*' I'd often heard Rose-ann say just those words.

Where was Rose-ann? Where was Ole Pa?

I was filled with wild sorrow that they thought me less than a dog. They both hated dogs.

I had to escape! I stood up. Where would I run? I ran nowhere.

Like an animal, I knew I must not leave the place my neglectful master—my blindness, had, not even bothering to chain, just left me.

The storm grew louder. Surely lightning had split the sky beyond repair.

The rain fell down. Was this a second flood? Had all the other people on earth been led into arks? Was I the only one forgotten?

All my life I'd had a fear bigger than myself, of storm. Never had I known one like this. I knew it was never going to end. Not until it had ended me!

Would the park cleaners sweep up my shrunken body? Wheel it away with the trash?

I began to cry as I'd never known a person could cry. I put my fingers into my mouth and shook my head this way, that way.

Sandwiched between two rolls of thunder I heard a pounding of footsteps coming down the path. They were not for me. Ole Pa could never run like that.

I knew that the footsteps belonged to a maniac—dreadful word!

'*An escaped maniac will creep up them stairs and grab you —wah! Grab you just like that—wahh! That's what's going to happen to you, any old day now. See if he don't.*' Sadie had told me this since forever.

The footsteps left the path. I heard them squishing over the sodden grass towards me—to get me.

I screamed loudly.

'Selina!' and Gordon caught me in his arms, against his strong, safe self.

CHAPTER FOURTEEN

I tried to burrow inside that strong safe Gordon. I kept on crying. I cried more than ever.

'Oh my *God!* Selina.' Gordon said the same words over and over, again and again.

He picked me up and carried me through the storm. The sound of the rain was different. It was beating on a roof.

'We are in a shelter,' said Gordon. I was sitting on a bench. I felt the rough wood with my wet hand. The wood was dry.

'Don't cry any more, baby. Don't cry any more, poor sad baby, don't cry any more.' Gordon knelt beside me.

He stood up suddenly and I heard him taking off his coat. 'I'm taking off my coat, Selina,' he said. He *told* me what he was doing.

His raincoat was cloth. The inside was dry and warm. I was wrapped in it. It was large and covered all of me. Gordon sat on the bench and dabbed at my face with his dry handkerchief. He brushed the wet hair from my face with his hand.

'Poor frightened, poor drowned baby,' he comforted. I was still crying but I was crying because he had come. It was too impossible, too wonderful that he had come. Things too too, are dangerous!

'You must stop crying,' said Gordon.

I stopped crying. Just like that. I began to make tiny breathless gulps. I couldn't stop. Every time I gulped my body jumped. I laughed.

'I can't stop gulping,' I said.

'You will. You will, honey.'

After a time I did stop. The rain still came down. It fell on the roof of the shelter. It seemed to me to be dancing on the roof. Had I ever heard a nicer sound?

'What made you come?' I asked.

Gordon's voice was unhappy. 'I don't quite know,' he said. Until that moment I had always in my thoughts thought of

Gordon as my friend. Mr Faber was my friend, Scum-dorg my dear animal friend. Had I really thought of Gordon as my friend? I knew he was my love.

Something in me, deep, deep in me, woke up. It had, without my knowing, been there ever since I'd been born, but sleeping, waiting.

Could Gordon feel my love?

'Is it dark, Gordon?' I whispered.

'It is dark,' he said.

'I'm glad.'

'Glad! Why, Selina? Why are you glad it's dark?'

'It makes you more like me,' I whispered. Gordon's voice was very quiet and low. The rain was louder than our voices.

'I can never be like you,' he said.

We sat, not talking. Then—so love is a pain, I thought. Had I ever felt such pain?

'The rain has stopped,' said Gordon.

'Yes,' I whispered. 'The rain has stopped.'

The rain had stopped very suddenly. The way people sometimes stop talking in the middle of a word. I wished it had not stopped.

'It's time for us to go,' Gordon stood up. He was, I could feel, in a hurry to go.

'Yes,' I said, 'it's time for us to go.' I stood up, draped in my borrowed coat. Such a big coat.

'Is there a step?' I asked.

'There are two,' said Gordon. He took my hand.

'Don't let go my hand,' I said.

'I won't.'

'I love you so much,' I said. I never meant to say those words. The words said themselves.

'So much,' I repeated.

'No,' said Gordon, 'no.'

'For ever and for ever and for ever,' I said.

'You are mistaken,' said Gordon, his voice full of pain. I couldn't bear the pain in his voice.

'I love you,' I said again. 'And I know—I know that you love me. You do. Don't you?' I whispered.

My feet made little sucking noises as I walked back to the tree. Gordon held my hand to guide me. The warmth and dearness had gone from his hand. It was the hand of a stranger, a stranger kindly helping a shiftless blind girl on her way.

'Love you?' asked Gordon. 'Why, Selina, I hardly know you. Here we are, under the tree again. Are you sure your grandfather will come to pick you up?' He gave me back my hand.

I was ashamed as I had never known to be ashamed.

I was—nothing. I had nothing, could do nothing—thread beads on strings, that was all. I was blind, unsightly . . .

What had got into me? I had told a man 'I love you' and, like a dish of cold unwanted food, my love was tossed back at me. Shame!

I began to speak in my thin high voice. 'Ole Pa! Sure, sure and he's bound to come soon. I'll never forget you coming to me in the storm. Wasn't it a dandy of a storm? I'm crazy to have been so scared. I've always been scared of storms. One would think I'd 've grown out of it by now. Time I grew up. I'll be fine now. I'll be O.K. now. Ole Pa is bound to come soon.'

My voice had never been so light, so thin and shallow.

'You are sure of that?' asked Gordon. He sounded weary —fed up and weary.

'Sure, he will come for sure,' I said.

As though I had a knowledge of things to come, we heard shuffling footsteps coming down the path. We heard Ole Pa's angry voice calling. Ole Pa was drunk.

'There's Ole Pa now,' I said.

'Sleena. You blind bitch! Slee-naa . . . ! Where are you? Sleenaa . . .' Ole Pa was good and drunk, falling over himself. How would we ever make it to the room?

'There's Ole Pa now,' I told Gordon in my light bright voice. 'Shikkered, for sure.' I sounded gay.

'Oh my *darling!*' said Gordon.

In his arms I heard the first words of love ever spoken to me.

All the love songs I'd ever listened to played in the night air of the park. Magic music . . .

Now I knew why all the radio dramas I had listened to kept a long moment of silence when the man said 'I love you.' The man in the drama was embracing the girl, the one he loved. Just as my love was embracing me. And I, at last and for ever, knew love.

'Oh my *darling!*' said Gordon.

Ole Pa was making a racket. 'Sleenaa . . . !' he yelled.

'Don't let him see us,' I whispered. Not that I cared any

more about Ole Pa, or anyone. I just didn't mean to have bad talk; any ugliness would spoil this moment.

Gordon felt like this too. He took his coat from my shoulders, and as Ole Pa crossed the grass towards me I called:

'Here! Here I am, Ole Pa. Over here.'

Gordon said: 'Oh my *God!*'

I never heard him go. I couldn't see him go, but I knew that he had gone.

'Here! Over here, Ole Pa.'

Ole Pa found me. We had a tough time getting back to the room. A tough time.

CHAPTER FIFTEEN

Rose-ann was in her bed. She'd no mind to worry about Ole Pa being so fall-down drunk. No mind to ask why I was so wet. Man! I was wet. Rose-ann was not working. It was one of her off-nights.

'Sleena,' said Rose-ann, 'I'm hung over. Fair hung over. Rub my back.'

'I'm wet, and cold. I'll rub your back soon's I'm good and dry, Rose-ann.' I went to the bathroom.

'Sleena, I want for you to rub my back now. I'm fair hung over—you hear me, Sleena?' I turned the water on and lit the heater.

'Sleena!' yelled Rose-ann.

Ole Pa thumped on the floor. He'd sat on the floor. Couldn't make it to his bed.

'Can it there! *Can* it!' yelled Ole Pa.

I turned off the heater and the water. It was better that I rub Rose-ann's back. Better any which way.

I rubbed Rose-ann's back. I'd not known she had got so fat. Since I was small Rose-ann had liked me to massage her. Man, she had got fat!

After a long time had passed by I was glad to hear Rose-ann snoring gently. Her snores were out of time with the loud snores of Ole Pa. They sounded funny. I giggled. Always these days I was laughing, crying, or giggling. These wonderful days.

I took off my wet clothes and crawled into bed. Like Rose-ann, I, Sleena, was 'hung over' too.

I knew that if I started to think I would never sleep. I must sleep. I must wake betimes. I never thought one thought. Too dangerous. I felt a smile steal over my—my 'heart-shaped face.' I knew why I was smiling. I fell asleep.

I can only tell that morning has come because I wake up. I wake up every morning with a happy heart. It takes a moment or two for me to settle down—to life. Takes time to remember that life is 'not all beer'n skittles.'

What, I wondered, was different about *this* morning? I knew! I knew for sure! but I was not going to think about anything. Not while Rose-ann was in shot of my thoughts.

I began to neaten up the room. I knew the room was a mess. I took our soiled yesterday's clothing into the bathroom, closed the door softly. I began to wash our clothes.

When Rose-ann was hung-over she slept good and hard. I knew I should call her. I didn't. I listened to Ole Pa's snores. 'Orrrr ker pooofuf!' On and on he snored.

I'd never worked so well. I'd a new sense of, relief, of importance. I was no longer—nothing! I was a girl—a real girl.

I turned on the bath water. When it was ready I got in carefully. Mustn't slip. Mustn't break my leg. I'd slipped once, a few years back, and broken my leg. The thought of doing that again didn't bear thinking of.

I knew I wouldn't look as nice to day as I'd looked yesterday. My blue blouse was wet. I'd have to wear the white blouse. The sleeves were too long but I'd roll them up. Might not look too bad. I sure hoped my grey cotton skirt was holding up, hoped it had no mark on it. If Rose-ann was not in too bad a mood I'd show her my shoes. Rose-ann had always brought me shoes. Her feet were bigger than mine.

My shoes were old and because they'd taken such a wetting last night they were hard and the toes were turned up. I worked them back'n forward, the way I'd worked my aching tooth back'n forward. I got them a bit softer. They felt queer, uncomfortable.

It didn't matter. I'd bigger things to worry about. I began to worry about Ole Pa. Would he take me to Park? Would he? Would he? He had to. But would he?

Ole Pa was about to wake up. He gave a snore so loud it made me jump. Woke him up. Woke up Rose-ann.

The room began to jump. The room had been very quiet except for Ole Pa's snores. It was crazy that two people could make such a rhubarb.

I gave up the idea of showing my shoes to Rose-ann and concentrated on doing things to please Ole Pa. I knew that if he got mad with Rose-ann he would be good to me.

He couldn't help his nature. I couldn't help *my* nature. I sure wished Rose-ann would do something about hers.

Ole Pa and Rose-ann had worked at the same place since for ever. Rose-ann had been at 'Ladies' since she'd been sixteen. Ole Pa had been at 'Mens' even longer. They'd seldom been late for work.

Because they were late awake this morning they took no note that I was bathed and dressed, that I'd been up and at it for hours, took no note of me at all.

'I'll put my face on at work.' Rose-ann drank down her coffee. 'You like I punch the clock for you, Ole Pa?' she asked.

Rose-ann sounded like Ole Pa was her dear father, like she cared about him no end.

What gets into people at times? Rose-ann was never good to Ole Pa.

Ole Pa was knocked flat by her kindness.

'You speak to me, Rose-ann?' he asked.

'You want I should punch the clock for you? I said shall I punch the clock? You like I punch the clock for you?' Rose-ann said patiently.

'Sure yes. Punch the clock for me. Sure good of you, Rose-ann.' Ole Pa, I knew, was scratching his head.

'I will,' said Rose-ann. 'I'll punch the clock for you. How can you get on time, poor you. How can poor old you get to work on time to punch the clock!'

'I done it all these long years,' said Ole Pa.

'I know. I know that for sure, Ole Pa. I know you punched that clock on time for ever. I know that.'

I heard Ole Pa scratching his head again. What had got into Rose-ann?

'What's got into you this morning, Rose-ann?' asked Ole Pa.

'Into me?' Rose-ann was very high tone. I didn't like it when she was high tone.

'Yes,' said Ole Pa. 'Into you?'

'If you can take a joke,' said Rose-ann, 'nothing got into me last night. I took myself easy last night. I feel good and rested, because, but nothing got into me last night.' She began to laugh.

'Nothing got into you last night?' Ole Pa sounded puzzled.

'Don't you dig me?' asked Rose-ann.

Suddenly Ole Pa gave a weird old laugh. A rusty cackling old laugh. Rose-ann and Ole Pa laughed together. I'd never heard them do this before.

'I dig you,' Ole Pa spluttered.

'Not bad, huh?' Rose-ann was that proud of her joke. 'Huh?'

'. . . but *good* . . .' Ole Pa couldn't stop laughing.

'Don't kill yourself, Ole Pa. It weren't that funny.'

Rose-ann I knew, had more to say to Ole Pa and he couldn't listen while he was laughing and she had no time to waste.

'You got no time to get to work on time if you going to take Sleena to the park. How can you take Sleena to the park and still get to work on time. I ask you?'

Rose-ann sounded like she was going to cry for the sadness of Ole Pa's life.

'What's that?' asked Ole Pa.

Rose-ann hated me for sure. I'd not known she hated me so much.

'You taking Sleena to the park?' asked Rose-ann.

'Like hell,' said Ole Pa.

'Like hell you *taking* her? Like hell you *not* taking her?" asked Rose-ann.

'Like hell—not,' said Ole Pa. 'An ole man like me. Thought I'd caught cold enough to die. Had to go to the park in the dead of night, in the raging wind and storm.'

'You shouldn't do it," said Rose-ann. "You shouldn't do it no more, Ole Pa.'

'I finished with all that baloney. Balls to all that hula-hula.' Ole Pa went to the bathroom and turned on the water.

'Good-bye, Sleena,' said Rose-ann.

'Good-bye, Rose-ann,' I answered her in a little voice. My voice sounded so little and sad I scarcely knew it.

I heard Rose-ann tip tap tip down the stairs. Ole Pa was singing while he shaved. I sat with a very straight back and my hands folded together. I listened to Ole Pa. I think he was happy because his kid, Rose-ann, had been nice to him.

'Pore ole monkey's dead,' he sang flatly.

'Cut his throat . . . with cake of soap . . . Pore ole monkey's dead . . . pore ole . . .'

Ole Pa stopped singing. He began to cough. He was unaccustomed to singing.

Was he going to take me to Park? He had to. He must. But was he?

I gave him his coffee. Sugared how he liked it. I polished his shoes. I guess they shone very brightly.

'You are going to take me to the Park aren't you, Ole Pa?' I asked.

'Hand me me denture, Sleena. I got to wash me denture. Pore-hore ole monkey's deh-heh-*hed* . . . Hand my dentures to me, Sleena.'

I gave Ole Pa his denture. 'You will take me, you are taking me, aren't you, Ole Pa?'

'Ask me again,' said Ole Pa.

'You are taking me?' I asked.

'Again. Ask me again.'

I could hardly speak from fear that he wasn't taking me.

'Will you take me, Ole Pa?' I whispered.

'No,' said Ole Pa. 'I finished with all that hula-hula.'

It couldn't be true. I listened to the door slam. I listened to Ole Pa's footsteps go along the hall. Go down the stairs. I *knew* that he would come back. Ole Pa didn't come back.

It was strange that I didn't cry. This, to me, was too big to cry over. I washed up the cups. Made Rose-ann and Ole Pa's beds. I put up the rope line in the bathroom and hung our yesterday's clothes out to dry. Then I got out my beads and began to work.

The 'milk had been spilt!'

I did the beads with all my might. With all my thought. I did this because I was good and scared of how I would feel if I thought about not going to Park.

I thought only about my work. It was too much. I tried too hard. Things too too, are dangerous! I should've remembered.

I couldn't keep it up. I knew that in the park, near by to the oak tree, Gordon would be waiting for me. I couldn't let him wait!

CHAPTER SIXTEEN

Last night, what had Gordon said to me? 'Oh my *darling*,' he had said . . .

'Oh my *darling* . . .' I cried out. 'I'm blind. I can't come to you. I'm *blind*.' I began to weep. Not cry. Weep.

I opened the door after a while. I'd stopped weeping. I opened the door and listened carefully.

If I asked someone to help me, would someone take me to Park? Would anyone?

I waited for someone to come out of one of the rooms. All day and every day, people were going in and out of their rooms. Times are I've been driven crazy with the banging of doors, the sound of voices and steps coming and going. I waited. No one came into the hall.

It was after one o'clock. The radio told me it was after one. Would Gordon still be there? Was he still waiting for me?

The door opposite our door opened. Mrs Favaloro came out of her room. I couldn't ask her. Mrs Favaloro was respectable. I knew that. A hundred times she'd yelled across the hall to Rose-ann, yelled at the top of her voice, told us that she was 'modesta . . . decente . . . respectable . . .' called us 'prostituta . . . immorale . . .' I knew that Mrs Favaloro was much too respectable to even listen to me. I shut the door to. Better not to let her see me.

Mrs Favaloro saw me. Before I could close the door entirely she called in her loud voice:

'I see you. Sporco! Dirty one! You think perhaps I am a man, a marito. Blind, oscuro, blind prostituta. I am no man. I know you. You do good to hide.' Mrs Favaloro rapped sharply on the now closed door. The door was old, but it was thick and strong. It was to me as though her sharp raps were on my face. I leant against the door. I could hardly breathe.

I would try to go to Park by myself! Why hadn't I thought of this before. There would be kindly people somewhere out in the city. Park wasn't far. Surely someone would help a blind girl.

I put on my sunglasses. I didn't want to show my loused up face, to spoil my chance of help. I took one of Ole Pa's white handkerchiefs from his drawer. Ole Pa only used white handkerchiefs. I don't know why I took this. I think I was thinking of the white flag of surrender. Soldiers in war, I knew, waved a white flag showing they had been defeated. I carried Ole Pa's handkerchief and went into the hall.

Since the rain had fallen, the weather had changed. All the bad smells in the world floated up the stairs and I felt scared.

I went back. I tried again. I took many more steps than anyone else to walk along the hall.

When I came to the stairs I waited hoping someone would come. No one came. I got down easier than I thought possible.

The air in the street was heavy, full of heat and humid. I used Ole Pa's hanky to wipe the sweat that fell down my face. Like tears! Like I was crying tears. Well I was. Only my tears fell in, not out.

To get to Park I knew I walked to the right, about forty steps. I walked, keeping close to the buildings.

After forty steps I knew the sidewalk ended.

The noise of traffic! The heat! The smells!

At the crossing I waited. A crowd of people gathered. I was among them. With no warning the people began to move. I caught hold of something. I was scared, but good.

'Watcha? Leave me be.' The man I'd held to shoved me off. I stumbled.

'Help me,' I said. 'I'm blind.'

'Says you.' That was that. I was touching other people. I moved among them.

'Are you sick, Honey?' someone asked me.

I said: 'No, blind. Help me over the crossing.'

'For sure.' A hand on my arm, and I was over the crossing. I wanted the owner of the helping hand to help me further. She had gone. Passed on. All the people in the street were in a hurry, like the rats were after them. Maybe all the people were blind! Maybe no one could see me. I didn't know if I was facing east or west. I didn't know where I was. I waved Ole Pa's handkerchief.

Another crowd of people gathered about and around me. Once more I was on the move with them. Jesus! I was crossing back the way I'd come! I was back on the side I'd started from. Was I? I didn't know. I didn't know. I was as wet from the heat as I'd been from the storm. I was dripping wet, from heat and fear.

Once again I caught up in a moving, pushing mob. I raised Ole Pa's hanky above my head.

'Help! Help me over,' I cried out. 'I'm blind.' Without a word spoken, a new hand took my arm and bustled me safely to the sidewalk.

Which side was I on now. I tried to remember. I couldn't. Was I on the side I lived on? I could not remember.

'Can you tell me if number seventy-three is this side?' I called out. Another crowd was beginning to gather.

'Is number seventy-three on this side?' I called out again.

People laughed. One person said:

'For sure. Seventy-three is this side.'

I caught hold of the one who'd spoken. I think it was the one who'd spoken.

'I'm blind, I can see nothing.' I was ashamed of the high pitch in my voice. My voice seemed to be sweating like my body.

'You've no right to be out alone.' A hand caught at my arm and took me to seventy-three.

'Seventy-three. Are you O.K.?'

'O.K., I'm O.K.,' I said.

'You've no right to be out alone,' scolded the voice.

Somehow I got upstairs, along the hall, into the room. I'd failed. Why had I tried? Hadn't I known I'd no right? No rights at all.

I should've known. I lay on my bed. I turned and lay on my stomach.

'Oh my *darling*,' I whispered. That's all I could think to say. I said it over and over.

I stayed on my bed for ever it seemed. I knew by the sounds about me that it was getting on to people's supper-time. I heard Mr Favaloro come home. I heard him giving a grand hullo to Mrs Favaloro. He banged his door shut.

The heat seemed to be growing stronger. I went to the window. The air was still and damp. In the street below I could hear children, screaming and playing, the way I always heard them. They sounded so all-fired happy I closed the window. I couldn't bear to hear happy people. Just like a tiger in a cage wouldn't care to see tigers out of a cage, jumping, slinking about through the uncaged world, I, in my cage of unhappiness, didn't care to hear the happy people.

Now it hit me! The day was over—I hadn't got to the park—I had missed being with Gordon. I couldn't take it!

Why should I have to take it? Did I have to? Was there nothing I could do about it?

I walked about the room I knew too well. I thumped when I spoke, thumped on the wall, on the table, like Ole Pa.

'Do I have to take this?' I yelled like Ole Pa.

Was this the way people went mad? Was I going mad?

'I am going mad,' I yelled. 'I know I'm going mad . . .'

I felt for sure that I was going mad. It was a bad feeling.

I began to call Ole Pa and Rose-ann all the dirty ugly words I knew, and I knew so many.

I used them on the people in the street, the thoughtless rushing people.

Who else did I know? Who else could I blame for my—for my tragedy?

I knew Gordon.

I began to cry. I crouched by the door and once again I called out. Not bad, not dirty words, but . . .

'Oh! My darling,' I cried.

I was too tired to get off the floor. I sat there for a long time. People passed along the hall. I'd never heard footsteps from this seat on the floor. How tired I was! Jesus! How tired and sad I was.

'Don't let Ole Pa, don't let Rose-ann come home till very late tonight, please God,' I prayed.

I had little left in me to face Rose-ann and Ole Pa with. I was a withered, dried-up thing.

And there was nothing I could do about it, nothing. Just like me, like Sleena.

CHAPTER SEVENTEEN

Someone knocked on the door. I'd heard no one come up the stairs. I hoped for sure, when I heard the knock, hoped it wasn't a friend for Rose-ann. Times are, I have a bad time explaining to Rose-ann's friends about the room down the hall.

'Who is it?' I asked.

'It is I, Yanek. I come with a message from my father.' The voice on the other side of the door was young, a happy voice. But who was his father? His father must be a strange man, sending his son to give a message to one like Rose-ann.

'Mrs D'arcey is not at home,' I said.

'Oh!' The voice fell. I imagined him as a fine son, glad to do as his father asked of him, disappointed to fail.

I opened the door. 'Write down the message if you wish. I'll give it to her. She comes in late.'

I could feel his eyes on my face. I wished I'd had on my sun-glasses. 'How old are you, Yanek?' I asked. I wanted to hear the fresh voice again.

'I am twelve.'

'You are tall,' I said.

'Pretty tall,' he answered proudly. He added: 'How do you know that I'm tall, a tall boy? You can't see, can you?'

'I can't see' I told him. 'But I can tell you are tall from the height of your voice.'

He gave a ringing laugh, 'That's keen,' he said. His voice grew a little distrustful. 'Why did you tell me you were not at home?'

'Your message is not for me,' I told him. 'Your message is for my mother.'

'Wow!' he said, and he sounded shocked. 'Is your mother blind too?'

'No.'

'Is your name Sleena?'

'My name is—yes, that's my name.'

Is the laughter of all twelve-year-old boys as sweet as the laughter of this one? I never heard a freer sound.

'My message is for you,' he laughed.

No one in the world had ever sent a message to me! I had to sit down.

'Who is your father?' I asked. 'Does your father know me?'

'For sure he knows you,' he comforted. 'Faber!'

'You are the son of my friend, of Mr Faber?'

'Sure am.' He was proud to be the son of Mr Faber.

'Was something wrong with the last lot of beads?' Jesus! I hoped not. I'd enough to stand up to without trouble from my work.

'The message doesn't mention beads or work. Puppa asked

me to say to you, he was sorry he was not able to bring the message. Too much work to do. Puppa works—but hard.'

'What is the message?' What could Mr Faber want to tell me? I was cold with the strangeness of having Mr Faber send me a message. 'Tell me,' I said.

'The message is, Puppa had a phone call from a friend of yours . . .'

Could it be? No, no, no, my thoughts interrupted Yanek's message.

'. . . from a Mr Ralfe . . .'

I put the tips of my fingers into my mouth and all of me went to my straining ears. I'd never listened so hard, so intently.

'Yes, go on.'

'He, your friend, asked Puppa to find out if you were sick. If you were not sick, he, your friend, would meet you to-morrow. Puppa said—your friend said—you would understand.'

'I do. Oh I do. I understand. It's a grand message. You gave it well, clearly.'

I decided to get the last second's joy from my dream.

'O.K.?' asked the vibrant voice of my dream messenger.

'Yes.'

'Then good-bye now.' He opened and shut the door. He had gone. I knew I was awake. I knew it for sure. I was scared to admit it. Too good. Too, too good!

Yanek Faber opened the door again. He didn't come in. He said:

'I almost gooffed! Puppa said he would be coming this way tomorrow. Had to walk through the park. Puppa said, would you care to go to the park?'

'Yes,' I said. 'Oh yes.'

'Then good-bye now,' said Yanek. His feet flew down the stairs. I knew that Yanek Faber was an angel. Humans can't fly.

I turned on the radio. A man was saying that soon a rocket was to be launched. It would reach the moon . . .

Silly boy! Silly boy! Why bother with the moon? It couldn't be as grand as here! I stopped his nonsense and turned the dial. 'In the shadows I will come and sing to you . . .' sang another man. Not in the shadows! In the bright tolerant open air of the park. I kissed my hands. I hugged my arms about Selina. It felt good to be near so happy a girl. Fine to kiss and hug the happiest girl in the world.

I did the coolest but craziest thing.

I opened the door and walked along the hall. I held on to the stair-rail and backed down the stairs.

'Hullo, beautiful world,' I called. Like a soldier, like a victorious soldier I walked along the sidewalk. The crowded sidewalk. I bumped hard into a fellow man.

'Woops!' I said.

'Same to you, doll,' laughed my fellow man. I stood at the crossing. A champing pushing darling crowd gathered. I wedged myself between it. Over we went! I came back wedged in another crowd. Soon I was back in the room. I hugged myself again. A fond happy hug.

I got to work. I wanted to be free, have everything good and neat. I was going out in the morning with my friend Mr Faber. He was taking me to Gordon.

CHAPTER EIGHTEEN

The heat of the day had got Ole Pa. He came back to the room poofed.

He was disappointed to find the room was hotter than outside.

'Man! This room ain't liveable. This room is but lousy with heat.' Ole Pa lay on his bed. '*Aaah*-hah-hah-haa *haaaa!*' He gave the biggest old yawn ever.

'You like I fix you a cold drink, Ole Pa?' I asked.

'Anything, anything, long as it's cold.'

I fixed a drink for him. When Ole Pa took his drink, he said:

'You got a forgiving nature, Sleena.'

'No,' I said, 'not really, Ole Pa.' I was thinking of how I'd lit into him and Rose-ann with all the dirt I knew.

'You have. A fine forgiving nature. You been in this sweat box all day, Sleena?'

Ole Pa was always asking me questions like this. He never

could take in that I was blind, couldn't see anything at all. I felt sorry for him. Old and hot, lying on his creaky bed in the room. I guessed that even Ole Pa had his dreams.

'It wasn't so bad,' I said. 'A breeze blew in betimes.'

'That's good. I'm glad there was a breeze.' Ole Pa went to take a bath. 'I'm getting out of here, can't stand this heat. Don't know how you stand it, Sleena.'

Before he went out to get shikkered, Ole Pa told me he'd brought home the provisions. Victuals he called the provisions.

'I brung the victuals, Sleena. I brung you some ice-cream. Put it to freeze.'

By this I knew Ole Pa felt a skunk about being the way he'd been to me in the morning.

'Thank you, Ole Pa,' I said. 'Thanks, I sure and for certain will relish some ice-cream. What flavour?' I could no more eat ice-cream than I could see it. I was going to make myself a cup of hot strong coffee. I knew Ole Pa would be glad if I asked him the flavour. I'd always like strawberry. He always brought strawberry and he always made me guess. It put value on his bringing it.

'Did you bring choclate?' I asked in a disappointed voice.

'Nope!' said Ole Pa triumphantly.

I went through the list.

'You don't know much,' said Ole Pa happily. 'I brung strawberry.'

'Strawberry! Wow!'

Ole Pa went out to get drunk. Poor old Ole Pa.

I made coffee. While I waited for it to perk, I washed a big helping of ice-cream down the sink—not that Ole Pa would ever notice, but how sad for him if by chance he did. Presents should be appreciated!

I ironed my blue blouse. I knew better than to think of tomorrow. My mind was sparkling with energy and it was hard to settle down. I settled down and listened to a big money Quiz. The only questions I missed out on were concerned with precious stones: gems. The correct answers were flattening to hear. I'd always thought of diamonds as being red; diamonds are not red. I listened to the answers. Now I'd always know how to describe precious gems even if I never had one or never really knew what they looked like. I could at least describe them. That could turn out handy—one never knew.

Rose-ann came in before the Quiz finished. She said she was but sick of life, up to her teeth, she was but sick of life.

'I'd like to go off on one of those cruises. Go on a big boat —sail away—never come back. Sail for ever on one of them big, rich boats. I'm fed up—but to the teeth,' said Rose-ann.

Then even Rose-ann had dreams. It was hard to think of Rose-ann dreaming. But here she was, dreaming.

'Rose-ann,' I said.

'You speak?' She was lying on her bed.

'Yes. Rose-ann, you get me on one of these radio quiz things. I know I'd win one. I'd give you the money and you could go on one of those cruises.'

'Hoo hoo! A fathead like you. Just what fill you with your crazy ideas? Did the acid rot your brain well as your eyes? Tell me that? Huh?'

I'd meant to be kind. I thought what a fine thing it would be to win a quiz and get shot of Rose-ann with the proceeds.

'Well?' asked Rose-ann.

'I don't know,' I said.

'*That*'s the way you'd answer Quiz questions. That's just for how you'd answer them. You know nothing—you are *nothing*. Jeeze! but I'm hung over. Rub my back, Sleena.' Rose-ann made a great noise turning on her stomach.

'Would you like to have a bath first, Rose-ann?' I asked. I should've known better. Man! Times are I ask for trouble.

Rose-ann was insulted. 'You saying I stink?' she asked. 'You saying I stink, Sleena?' I knew she was going to sock me and I knew if she missed it would make her madder. I was going to be socked anyway. Rose-ann had the advantage of being able to see where I was. If I ducked she'd come after me. Her temper would be stronger, so would her arm.

Rose-ann socked me. Right on the puss. I sucked a trickle of blood into my mouth. Salty! Just like tears.

'Rub my back, Sleena.' I rubbed her back.

CHAPTER NINETEEN

Ole Pa and Rose-ann dragged off to work. It was a hot steamy morning for sure.

Man! I felt sorry for both of them.

I drank my coffee slowly and with relish. The radio was playing suitable music for my mood. Me, with a mood!

I was a spoilt and pampered star. No one was more pampered than me. I knew this. I'd never known such a feeling. My feelings were so deep, so thankful.

I heard Mr Faber coming upstairs. I opened the door to him.

'Good morning, Mr Faber,' I said. 'You are so kind.'

'Nah! Not kind! Shust I was coming this *vay*. Good mornink, Sleena. You look luffly!'

'Thank you, Mr Faber. I feel lovely too.'

'I am glat—glat you are harpy. You think my Yanek is goot boy, yes?'

'I do. Oh I do. What a fine boy you have, Mr Faber.'

'Neffer no man had *viner*,' Mr Faber said proudly. We were a mighty happy pair, Mr Faber and I.

I told him how I'd tried to get to Park yesterday. Told him how I'd so much wanted to go and couldn't.

'You dried to valk arlone! Vonderful! Vine! You are vonderful.'

'Oh no, Mr Faber,' I said, 'not wonderful.'

'Vonder*ful*,' he insisted. Maybe he was right. Man! What had got into me? Thinking like that. I'd better draw my horns in.

We walked into the heat. Mr Faber carried my boxes. Soon we were in Park. It was no cooler.

'You vant same place to sit as bevour, Sleena?'

'Yes please, Mr Faber.'

I was beneath the oak tree again. Could it be true? It was true.

'Will you put the boxes just here,' I told Mr Faber.

'No,' he said, 'you do no vork today. No vork art tall.'

'No work! I must do the beads. I'm back with them.'

'No matter. No vork today. I, Faber, take the boxes to home. Stepha, my girl, vill do them.'

'But—Mr. Faber . . . Rose-ann will know . . .'

'Vill know! Ow?'

'The—money.'

'She vill never know. I make gift to my best vorker—to you, Sleena.'

'Oh Mr *Faber*!' I was deeply moved.

'I go now, Sleena. When does he come?'

'Who, Mr Faber?'

'Sleena! You play joking with Faber. I ask ven does he come? Your boy-frient.'

'Oh!' I felt my face grow slowly warm.

'Ah-haa! Oh! Oh-hoh!' Mr Faber began to laugh. Jesus! I wish Mr Faber was my father instead of Harry.

'Look about, Mr Faber,' I said. 'He may be here now.'

'Vat is he looking like, Sleena?'

Gordon! What did he look like. How could I describe him to my friend. I knew what Gordon was like, but not what he looked like.

'He, he is six feet tall,' I said proudly. 'He has a deep quiet voice, the kindest voice . . . his hands are gentle, strong . . .'

'Vait, vait! From all this I know but only he is six feet tall.' Mr Faber I knew was looking about him. 'No, Sleena. I can see a few people, your boy-frient has not yet come.'

'He will come,' I said.

'He vill come—vor sure.' Mr Faber took my hand in his. His hand was dry and rough, but so kind.

'I go now,' he told me. 'I haff to valk again through bark. I valk here at six by the clock. You vant I valk you to home, Sleena?'

'Please. Yes please. Mr Faber you are the best man in the world.'

'Nah!' Mr Faber told me good-bye and I was alone. I pressed my face against the trunk of the oak tree. I felt with my hand to where I had buried my treasure. I must ask Gordon the words of the sad little song my music-box had played. So many things to ask, to tell, to do and feel . . . No work to do!

CHAPTER TWENTY

Perhaps being blind, because it takes away the sense of seeing, perhaps it gives another sense in its place. A sense of knowing things, of being aware.

I knew that Gordon was near by, that he was looking—at me. I knew it for sure. I wondered why he sat a way off. Why he didn't come over to me. Didn't he know how much I wanted to be with him?

I waited as long as I could. I could wait no longer. I waved my hand. Waved it in a circle. I wasn't sure which direction to wave to.

'Gordon!' I called. I hadn't meant my voice to sound so little.

Gordon must have been very near. In an instant he was sitting beside me.

'Oh my *darling*,' he said. There were tears in his voice. In mine too.

'You were watching me,' I said.

'Yes. I was watching you.'

'But why?'

He was silent; then he said: 'I'll tell you another time. You tell me, you tell me why you were unable to come yesterday. Why, Selina?'

To be called Selina, again. The wonder of it!

I told him about my day—my bad day. When I told him about thumping and yelling bad words he held my hand and I was safe from all bad things.

Gordon never spoke at all. Not words. I felt his hand on mine. When I'd finished my story my hand was buried in the warm shelter of Gordon's hand. I wanted to leave it there for ever.

'. . . and here I am,' I finished up, 'with you.'

'Yes,' he said.

'My day—my day of love,' I said.

'Is that what today is to you?' Could it be that his voice had toothache—this happy day?

'Selina—does today mean so much to you?' he asked again. His voice *was* unhappy. Why—why?

'Yes,' I said. 'Not to *you?*' I asked. I was scared. I knew I sounded scared.

Gordon laughed and took my hand again.

'It's the most wonderful day in all the world,' said Gordon.

I was happy again. 'I can't believe you love me—that I love you,' I told him. He squeezed my hand.

'Don't you feel good? Don't you feel well, Gordon?' I asked. He was so quiet. 'Is it the heat?'

'It must be the heat,' he told me. The heat *was* bad. I could hardly draw a clear breath myself, and I'm used to the heat.

'Selina.' Gordon spoke quickly. 'Is there a chance that Mr Faber will come for you before five o'clock?'

'No chance,' I said.

'Well then! Would you care to come to my apartment? It's very near by. It's cool and pleasant. Will you come, Selina . . . ?'

Would I go to Gordon's apartment? I'd never been to anyone's apartment!

'Ask me again!' I said boldly.

'Will you come, Selina?'

'Yes. Yes, yes,' I told him.

'Then,' said Gordon, 'let's go.' He took my two hands in his and I was on my feet like never before. 'How'd I get up like that?' I laughed.

'That was easy,' laughed Gordon. He sounded happier. I knew it had been the heat worrying him. We were leaving the hot Park. He was feeling happier.

I held back in fear when the cab pulled up.

'No,' I said. 'I'm frightened. I've never been in a cab.'

'Please. Just get in, Selina,' Gordon's hand was strong on my arm.

'I will,' I said. 'I will. Just give me time.'

'There's no time. We're holding up traffic.' Gordon's voice was deep and low.

'Anything wrong there? Anything wrong, ma'am?'

The cab-driver had called me—ma'am. I couldn't believe it.

'Nothing's wrong,' said Gordon. 'Get in, Selina.'

I got in. I was sorry to have been such a baby. The cab was fine. I'd have liked a longer drive.

We got out again. 'Sure everything's O.K., miss?' the cab-driver asked me again.

'Fine. Everything's but—fine,' I told him happily.

'One never knows,' said the driver. He drove off noisily.

Gordon led me into his apartment building. I knew it was better than our building at once. I could tell. I got a bad scare. A bad one. I heard a door open. I went through the door. Holy cats! The door shut and my stomach went turning over—up to my neck and down to my boots. 'Man!' I cried out.

'Selina. What the—what's wrong?' asked Gordon.

'Where are we? What's happening?' I cried.

'I'm sorry. I'm sorry, baby. I should have told you. Haven't you been in an elevator before?'

'No,' I said. 'Is this an elevator?' I was glad for sure it was an elevator. I'd thought the floor was falling . . . and yet we were going up? Strange! Wonderful!

'I'm sorry, honey.' Gordon held my hand. If he'd been holding my hand all the time I wouldn't've been scared at all.

We walked along the hall.

'This is the hall,' he told me.

'Just a moment, Gordon,' I said. I bent down and felt the floor. Carpet in the hall! How *'bout* that!

'Jesus! Carpet in the hall,' I said. Gordon laughed so loud I was nervous.

'Don't. Don't laugh so loud.'

He laughed still, but softly. 'You,' he said, 'are too dear to live.' That's exactly what he said.

I heard him open the door. A cool wall of air was in front of me. I stepped back a little.

'The apartment is air-cooled,' he told me.

'Is it?' I asked in wonder. 'Does it cost very much?'

'Not much.'

'You must be rich.' I hoped Gordon wasn't rich.

'I barely make ends meet.' Gordon laughed again. He shut the door.

'Are you here alone?' I asked.

'I live with my brother. My brother Paul. He is at his work. He is a doctor. Three years younger than me.'

'And not half as nice,' I said firmly.

'He wouldn't agree with you.'

'He's a silly boy,' I laughed.

I asked Gordon to tell me about the room. He took me walking through the cool, clean air, over the soft carpet. I felt the books. So many books. I sat on the divan. So big, so silently bouncing. I bounced up and down.

'What a fine place,' I said.

'Selina, it's a simple place,' said Gordon.

'It's a very fine place. Where do you cook? Do you have a bathroom? We have a bathroom. Do you sleep in this room? Where is your bed?'

'Hold your horses. I'll take you on a grand tour. I'll take you all over.'

Gordon took me all over. I was flattened. Not only this room. Two rooms to sleep in. One for Gordon, one for brother Paul. A bathroom that smelt so fresh and good I would've liked to stay there for ever. A separate room to cook in. Such madness. Such wonderful madness.

'Are you sure you're not very rich?' I asked.

'Quite sure.'

'Man! Do other people live like this?'

'Millions live much better, but much.'

'Man!' I was flattened for real. 'Man!' We went back to the first room.

'Are there flowers in this room?' I thought I could smell roses—like in the park.

'There *is* a bowl of roses.'

Flowers! In the room! How '*bout* that?

'I knew it!' I followed the scent. Yes, roses. 'Are they red?' I asked.

Gordon hesitated, then: 'Yes,' he said.

'I don't think they are red,' I said.

'The roses are white,' he said slowly.

'They must be beautiful. Gordon—why did you say they were red?'

'I'm sorry, Selina. I was wrong. I thought, as you know the colour red . . . I thought you would enjoy the roses more . . .'

'You were being kind! Don't ever tell me anything not true about feelings . . . thoughts . . . or the colour of things. Isn't it cruel to be kind—sometimes?'

'Very, most cruel. Sometimes also . . . it's kind to be cruel.'

'That I do not hold with. Not at all. That I don't like

. . . promise you won't be cruel to be kind . . . promise you won't be—most of all—kind to be cruel . . . promise, promise . . . ?'

'I never make promises. I don't like . . .'

'Then just for today? Just for this, my wonderful day? Tomorrow—anything! Promise?'

'For today, for today then I promise.' Gordon promised.

I knew that my day was safe. I was alone with Gordon for the first time. We had never been alone in the park! I knew that now.

Now that we were alone, why didn't Gordon hold me in his arms? That was where I wanted to be. Nowhere else. Didn't he want to touch me? Hold me? In the cab I'd reached for his hand, Gordon had put my hand back on my lap. Didn't lovers hold hands in cabs? I knew that they did.

Something was just not right. I remembered the sweetness, the wild mad sweetness, after the storm had passed away. I thought of the words, thought of the feelings that had—sure as I know God—been felt by me, yes, and by Gordon. What was wrong?

'You don't really love me, do you?' I asked. Before he could answer I cried:

'No no, don't answer *that*. You are unhappy about something?' Once more I cried: 'And don't answer *that*. Tell me nothing is wrong, tell me everything is fine . . . You won't break your promise if you tell me that; everything is fine. It is. It *is*.' I added a whisper: 'Isn't it?'

Gordon's laugh was lovely to hear. I knew that everything was fine, going to be finer. I laughed too.

'You are the most impetuous girl. Tell me, don't tell . . . do, don't . . . Come here, Selina, sit here.'

We sat on the bouncy divan. I gave a tiny bounce.

'Quit that, you baby. Selina, this is a fine and happy day. I want you to have a day, a day fit for an eighteen-year-old girl. A fine, happy day. Do you understand me?'

'A fine happy day,' I mocked. 'I love you. Can I have a fine happy day when you won't even kiss me—when I'm going to die if you don't—I'm going to die right here, right now, on this fine bouncy seat if you don't kiss me. Don't you want to kiss me? Don't answer *that*. Please kiss me and let me live and have a fine happy day . . .' I stopped to draw breath.

'I'm glad I have that bowl of roses,' said Gordon. 'When

you are, when you have "passed on" I shall cover you with the petals. It seems a shame though to die at only eighteen.' He laughed, but mournfully.

'Then you aren't going to kiss me?' I couldn't bear that he didn't want to.

Gordon took both my hands and I was on my feet again, using his strength, not mine, like in the park.

'For Pete's sake!' he said, 'you are shameless.'

'Yes. Shameless!' I said.

'Are you going to behave yourself?' he teased. Wonderful to be teased.

'Never! Not until I have been kissed. By you,' I added.

Gordon was still holding my hands. I felt as if we were miles apart. Were his arms made of steel? I wondered. Suddenly he bent his head and I felt his lips brush the tip of my nose.

'You have been kissed,' he said lightly and he let go my hands.

I could see nothing but I knew that one step and I could be where I wanted so much to be and where I knew, knew I was wanted. I could have been in Gordon's arms. The wisdom that God gives—does God give it? Whatever and whoever gives it—held me back. I laughed because I knew he wanted as much as I the same thing. I wanted. I laughed because I was so all-fired happy. Just like a girl of eighteen ought to be.

'Was that a kiss, Dad?' I asked, and poked my face forward.

'That was a kiss, Dad.' Gordon picked me up like I was a feather and he walked a way and dumped me down.

'You are now sitting on a table, a high table in my kitchen. No funny business, or you are due for a fall. You dig me, baby, huh?' He was playing gangsters.

'Dig,' I said through the corner of my mouth. He laughed again. The cool, cloudless day began.

'What would you like to drink—cold, hot?'

'Hot—wonderful hot coffee,' I said. The coffee was the best coffee in the world.

I found out so many things that first day in Gordon's air-cooled apartment. I found out that if you liked a special song, special music, you could buy a disc, play it yourself, on a record player. Any time you wanted to.

No need to wait till it came over the radio! Play it over and over, any time you felt like it. Man!

I found out how better food tasted when it was prepared for you, served in smooth nice dishes, eaten with a silver fork . . . how handy a linen table napkin could be. I drank iced soup!

After we'd eaten and neatened the kitchen. (I'd've given a year of life gladly to have seen that fresh nice kitchen.) After that we went and played more records; played them softly, far far away music, the music *I* had asked for. We played them softly so we could talk. We sat on the divan and we talked of many things. I asked question after question. I got an answer for each one. Man, oh man!

Gordon told me about the way I should be learning to read, write (me—reading and writing!) He told me stories about people, blind people, who'd even written books.

That was going a bit far.

'That's hard to believe,' I said. '*That's* going a bit far.'

He brought a book from the many books I'd felt in the room.

'Hold it in your hands, Selina.' I held the book. 'This book was written by a woman who was blind. Who could not hear. Who could not speak.'

'How did she do it?' I asked in wonder. He told me. I felt like a bee. Flying from flower to flower, gathering the sweet honey of knowledge. Never was there a hungrier, harder working bee than me, Selina. Never a better bush than Gordon, offering the honey-filled flowers for me to drink from.

Each minute of that day was an hour, but then every hour as it finished was but a minute.

When my records were finished, Gordon stacked the music he liked best on the player. I had asked questions, talked through my records. During Gordon's music I hardly spoke at all.

As time went by I became part of the music. Inside the music. I put out my hand and Gordon held it in his. I moved a little closer and my 'pale gold head' rested on his shoulder.

Then this is love! I thought.

Together, music, quiet and peace, hands clasped and head on the shoulder of the loved one. So this, too, was love.

I fitted my thoughts to soft sweet sadness that floated about us . . .

'It is dark! I cannot see,' cried my heart.

'Selina, take my hand,' the answer came to me, and I thought: Now I am safe, no need to see, but—I am weary . . .

'Selina, lean your head upon my shoulder . . .'

So this was love! I was truly full of wonder.

This I knew was a day that should have lasted for ever.

When the music had finished, I told Gordon what I'd been thinking. About the way I felt. He understood and he told me that every person in the world felt as I did.

'People are like vines, Selina. We are born and we grow. Like vines, people also need a tree to cling to, to give them support.'

'Even you?' I asked.

'Yes indeedy! Even, and very much so—I,' said Gordon. 'Everybody.'

'I'm glad to know that,' I said.

I knew that time was passing. I was scared that when five o'clock came I would crumble up and fall into little broken pieces. I was scared for sure about when five o'clock would come.

CHAPTER TWENTY-ONE

Paul came before five o'clock!

Gordon had gone to shower and change. To get ready for his work. I felt sorry that I couldn't be with him. I knew though, even though I couldn't see, that it wouldn't be fitting. I sat holding the book that had been written by a person that couldn't hear or speak . . .

Paul came into the apartment and the still cool air began to whirl with his movement and energy. I knew it was Gordon's brother because of his voice. The same, although not so deep—but oh, the dizzying speed of those words.

I stood up when he came in. I'd never met anyone before, not really.

'How do you do?' I said. 'I'm Selina D'arcey.'

'Hullo. Can I help you? Are you selling something? Are you a census-taker? What brings you here? Have you seen my brother? I gather you must have, otherwise you'd not be sitting here. I'm open to any questions. What is it you want to know? Are you one of those people who works for societies who like to know how the rest of the world lives? I assure you I know the answer to every question ever thought up by such societies. Shoot! No? Then you must be selling something . . .'

I'd not known a human could speak so fast. As he spoke he moved about the room. I heard him change the records. He started the player. Bam! The music blared wildly.

I told him I wasn't selling anything. He came closer to me. 'Selling what?' he asked loudly.

My mind was pounding like the drums in the music. I pointed to the record player and shook my head.

'You don't like it? Too loud? You're so right.' He snapped it off.

'Now! that's better. What was it you said you were selling?'

'Nothing,' I said.

'Not selling anything? No? Then . . .'

'I'm your . . . I'm Gordon's friend,' I told him quietly.

He didn't speak for a long time. Then he spoke faster than ever.

'I beg your pardon. I'd no idea. I do beg your pardon. Sit down—please sit down. You must be lenient with me. Missed out on my sleep. Strange thing, but if I miss out on sleep for play I don't notice. Miss out because of w ... That's the least . . . You agree?'

Man! Why did he have to talk so fast? He sounded like the rats were after him for sure. Sounded like he had no time to get where he was going, but was determined to get there anyway. He rattled on.

'I see you don't agree. That rates. That figures. Gordon's friends never do agree with me. Can never understand me. It's sad but true. It's sad isn't it?'

I knew by his voice that he was smiling. I smiled to where I thought he was standing when he spoke. I was going to answer him but he went on faster than ever.

'I'll go and dig Gordon out for you. I'll tell him what poor manners he has. His manners are extremely poor. I'll see

what he's up to. I'm sure he's up to no good. He's a man
without social grace. Now I have beautiful manners. You
agree? I see that you don't. Excuse me.'

The room felt empty. I listened and heard his quick tense
voice speaking with Gordon.

'Is that you, Paul?' Gordon asked.

'But of course. Excuse me for asking, Dad, but what gives?
What gives out there with Orphan Annie, with little Eva.
With your—friend—so I'm told. You care to tell me what
gives, Dad? Honoured older brother, you mind telling me
about this friend of yours?'

Was he being rude about me? I wasn't sure. I heard Gordon laugh. Then, he wasn't being rude. He'd told me Gordon's friends never understood him. I would understand him.
What was Gordon saying?

'You look beat up. Why don't you get more sleep. You'd
better hit the sack. Why don't you slow down, man? You
need to slow down.'

'It's nice to know you care. I'm glad you love me, Dad.' I
heard them laughing together. It was fine to hear brothers
laughing together. Paul went on speaking.

'You're evading the issue—I don't like any issue being
evaded. What gives with li'l Eva? Who, what, when, where,
and for Pete's sake, why? Why?'

Gordon's voice was slower, deeper than ever. So different
from his brother's.

'What did Selina tell you?' he asked.

'Selina? Of course, Selina. Selina told me she was a friend
of yours . . .'

'That's right.'

'You snubbing me, Dad?'

'Could be,' laughed Gordon. 'Take it or leave it.'

'I'll take it. I'm not like you. I don't mind a snub. I just
don't like not knowing what goes on. Where did you meet
this . . .'

'Selina.'

'Thanks. Selina. Where did you meet her?'

'I met her in the park.'

'Bro-theer!' Paul sounded but surprised, upset! 'I don't
bring home gals I pick up in the . . . anywhere. I never
knew you picked up girls. When you start picking up girls?'

'I haven't started.' Gordon sounded unhappy. 'Paul, I'll lay
this out for you later on. Selina is blind. She needs help . . .'

'Maybe. Maybe she needs help, but not as much as you, man. You need help . . .'

'I don't need help. I know where I'm going . . .'

Paul interrupted. He spoke a little slower.

'Well,' he said, 'just so long as you're not asking for trouble.'

'You know me, you know me, Paul. Have I ever asked for anything else?'

'You speak the truth, oh brother.' Paul I knew, gave a yawn. 'God! how tired I am. I am but tired. Trouble I don't mind. Most kinds of trouble I don't mind. Some kind of trouble I *mind*.'

'Me too,' said Gordon. 'You're way off the beam. I don't intend to have trouble, not the kind you're hatching up.'

'Gals is trouble. Big, small, any gal, discount what they look like. Discount size, colour, shape—gals is trouble. And this gal . . .'

'You disillusioned old bum,' laughed Gordon. 'Have a shower, take a powder, hit the sack.'

He was still laughing when he came and joined me.

'That was Paul,' he told me and his voice was but proud.

'No kidding?' I teased.

He laughed. 'Paul thinks he's one great ball of fire.'

'And you! What do you think of him?'

'I think he's one great ball of fire.'

'I thought that was what you thought of him.'

Gordon sat beside me. He smelt wonderful. He lit a ciga-rette and the smell of the smoke and the smell, fresh and bathed, of Gordon made my stomach turn right over. It turned right over. I was surprised and felt just like I had in the elevator, only much nicer—much.

'My stomach turned upside down just now,' I told Gor-don.

'Lord! Are you going to be sick?' he asked.

I laughed—I was so happy. 'No,' I said. 'It turned over because I am near you again and you smell so all-fired nice.'

'You are a baby. Only a baby would talk to a man like that. If your tummy turned over, I don't wonder. Too many cold and hot drinks.'

'Think that if you please,' I said. 'I know better.'

Gordon was silent. I was sorry I'd spoken to him about my inside.

'Excuse me.'

'Umm?' Gordon sounded far away and very grown up.

'Excuse me for speaking of my inside,' I said.

'Your——' I loved his quiet laugh. 'Selina,' he told me, 'I'm sure you have a very nice inside. You can talk about anything in the world to me, it's just that my mind is on other things.'

In a flash of time all my happiness went, and it was dreadful the way I suddenly knew how unimportant a person I was.

The wonderful day in the untrue cool air, the smoothness of things, the freshness I had smelt all day, had frozen my memory.

I felt it unfreezing. Soon I would be back in the heat, the heavy smells I'd grown up with, the sleezy rough life of the room and I would smell the likker on Ole Pa.

Smell and hear the person Rose-ann, my mother, was.

I wished I'd never come with Gordon to his home. Wished I'd never heard two brothers talking and laughing—caring together. I wished I'd died a long time back.

I folded my hands together and my chin rested on my chest, all folded up. Like a dying flower—not dead, but worse, dying.

'I don't know how I'm going to do it,' Gordon said, suddenly, 'but somehow, someway, I'm getting you away from Rose-ann, from . . .'

Quickly, like a change of radio stations, my hands were clasped beneath my high-held chin. I was smiling into the air about me.

'Was your mind on other things—about *me*?' I whispered.

'But of course.' Gordon went on telling what he was thinking about. It was all about me. I felt like the crispest, craziest, most scenty flower that ever was. 'Tell me, tell me,' I begged.

'You can't go on living the way you are. I can't believe you've been so overlooked. It's a dark-age story.'

'I certainly can't go on,' I said.

'I'm going to need help,' said Gordon. 'But who?'

'Yes,' I said. 'Who?'

'It's a touchy, a delicate situation.'

'It is,' I said. 'It certainly is,' he went on, as though he hadn't heard me.

'I'll have to be more than careful.'

'Very, very careful,' I agreed.

Gordon laughed and I lost one of my hands. It was swallowed up in his warm dear hand.

'Selina,' he said to me, 'you—you're so darned sweet.'

I never meant to do what I did but just like a young child I moved and pushed my way into his arms. Not like an eighteen-year-old girl in the arms of the man she loved but like a little girl in the arms of a person who cared about her.

Gordon held me against him. His arms went around me and I felt his cheek against mine. He held me like this for just the quickest moment but it was for ever and the dearest moment of my life.

I felt Gordon's hand pass over my hair. Then he swung me like a puff of air on to my feet.

'Time to go.' Raising his voice he called: 'We're off, Paul.'

Paul came into the room. He smelt as fresh and fine as Gordon. Lighting a cigarette he came up close to me. My stomach didn't even quiver. Now that he knew I was blind he spoke slowly, like my ears were bad too.

'So you're off. I'm sorry you have to be off. I would like to talk to you.' I put out my hand and he held it just for a second. His hand was narrow and nervous.

'Good-bye,' he said again.

I said good-bye to him. We went from the cool air into the warm air of the hall.

Paul spoke so quickly, so quickly, after his slow talk, I got a shock.

'Sure you can see the forest? Sure that the trees aren't stopping you from seeing the forest?'

'What did you say?' I asked.

'Paul is talking to me,' said Gordon. 'Paul, hit the sack. I've lived in the forest for years, man. I'm part of the forest. Hit the sack—sleep. You need sleep.'

'You are so right,' answered Paul. He closed the door. Closing me out of the day, my wonderful day.

'I'm late,' Gordon told me.

CHAPTER TWENTY-TWO

When I was sitting beneath the oak tree alone I knew exactly how a millionaire must feel on losing his fortune, and I felt lousy, the way he would feel.

The heat of the day seemed to have gathered in a lump, and settled beneath the branches. I rested my head against the trunk and tried to forget I was alive, but I couldn't.

I tried to remember the day I'd lived through—clean dear day! Although it was still day, and I was not asleep, my thoughts were like a bad dream. I could remember only the sad, the cruel and ugly things in my life.

It was like Sadie was talking to me, telling me about Harry, about how I wouldn't be blind if Harry hadn't come to the room unexpected that night.

I'd always accepted that he had come back unexpected— I'd never blamed either Harry or Rose-ann. Just I was blind. That was that!

I thought of how I'd been happy when I met Pearl. How I'd been excited knowing a little girl.

Just my luck I thought—I would have a murderer for a father, a whore for a mother, a shikkered old bum for a grandfather, a dirt black nigger girl for the only friend I ever met. Just my luck to have a loused-up face, unseeing eyes, burnt out eyes (I wondered what colour my eyes *had* been).

My life was disgusting.

I'd even been raped by a casual customer of my mother's. The thought, the memory of that time seemed to hit me for the first time.

I'd just accepted it before. I'd been 'done over.' That was that!

Why couldn't Harry have come home like other fathers?

Why hadn't Rose-ann been waiting for him, mad with happiness because her husband was home from the war?

Why wasn't Ole Pa a man who could live without getting drunk every night of his life?

Gordon laughed. 'You are cute, Selina D'arcey.' He laughed again. I felt foolish, confused.

'Why do you laugh?' my voice was deep.

'Ahh!' he copied my voice. 'Let me laugh, you sounded so knowing, so experienced, you—baby!' he said. Gordon thought I was showing off. I never showed off. He should show more—more tolerance towards me.

'I am no baby, Gordon,' I said, my voice had never been so deep. 'I've been—laid. I've been done over,' I told him, in my deep voice.

'What did you say?' The way Gordon asked me that, was as if I'd said: 'I killed Mr Faber and Scum-dorg yesterday, Gordon.' I told him again.

Gordon didn't say a word. Was he laughing silently? Did he think I was showing off?

'Gordon?' I said.

He didn't answer me. He did think I'd been lying, showing off. He was despising me.

I told him about Rose-ann and Harry again. Told about Rose-ann and her friend. About how Rose-ann had been locked out in the hall. In plain clear words I told Gordon about me and Rose-ann's friend—about that night.

Still he didn't answer me. What was the matter?

'Is anything—wrong with you, Gordon?' I asked.

I felt uneasy. It's bad when people don't answer, when you're blind.

'Wrong with me? No,' said Gordon.

I'd cried too often myself not to know by their voices when people cried.

Gordon was crying. I knew men seldom cried. I'd listened to so many radio dramas, stories. 'And John, his head buried in Veronica's lap, cried the dreadful tears of a strong man . . .'

Only last week during the Faith for Today half-hour, the Pastor had said: 'And Jesus wept!'

Jesus had been a man when he had lived on this earth.

In the radio story John had wept because he'd been unfaithful to Veronica and Veronica had found out about it.

Jesus had wept for love, for the loss of his friend.

What was Gordon weeping for? Had he pricked his finger? I knew it hurt like hell when the needle went in deep.

'Did you prick your finger, Gordon?' I asked. 'Is that why you are weeping?'

'Yes,' said Gordon.

'Suck it,' I said. 'Suck it good'n hard.'

'Thanks! I will,' said Gordon. He didn't though. I didn't hear a thing.

I was sorry he had hurt himself, but in a way I was glad for here was my chance to know whether it was true or not that the tears from crying tasted of salt. 'Salty tears fell down the smooth curves of Veronica's cheeks . . .'

'Excuse me, Gordon,' I said. 'Owing to the acid that burnt out my eyes, when I cry I do not shed tears. Would you let me have one of yours?'

'In God's name, why?' asked Gordon.

Had I done a bad thing in asking him?

'I have never felt a tear. I've heard so much about them. Do you mind?'

'In God's name, no,' said Gordon. 'Here! Help yourself.'

Gordon had never touched me before. I had never touched Gordon. He guided my hand to the place on his face where I could catch one of his tears. His hand was strong and very friendly.

I was surprised. I had been sure tears were little crystals, like salt. They were water!

'Is this a real tear?' I asked.

'Real—for sure,' he told me.

Before the tear dried up I flicked at it with my tongue.

'It's true,' I said.

'In God's name, why did you do that?' asked Gordon. 'What's true?'

'Tears do taste of salt,' I laughed.

Gordon asked me: 'Do you remember the Chinese song I said for you yesterday, Selina?'

'Sure,' I said. To show him how well I remembered it I said it through.

'. . . Long lotus, short lotus,
　　　　Cook it for a welcome,
　　　　And be ready with bells and drums
　　　　For the pure-hearted girl.'

I finished up proudly. I was always feeling proud these days.

'You knew it before,' said Gordon.

'Before what?'

'You'd heard it—the poem before—before.'

Why couldn't Pearl have been a nice little white girl? Why, why, why?

Why couldn't it have been a man I loved—who loved me? Why had my decency, my pride as a girl, a woman, been torn so savagely by an unknown marauder? Why, why and oh why?

After the day I'd just spent, why did I have to think only of these dreadful things? Was I born with a wicked heart? Was I always being punished for my born wickedness? Would it turn out that meeting—knowing, yes and loving Gordon would follow on, turn out not to be fine, clean and wonderful?

Sitting under the tree, thinking over my life, I couldn't figure out how anything good, lasting good, could be for me.

I listened to the passing footsteps of seeing people, heard the murmur of voices, heard laughing voices, angry, tired voices. I'd 've changed my life with any of those passing people, taken a long shot, become any one of them.

I tried to remember myself back to the cool apartment, to hear the slow loved voice of Gordon. The air, like a cold wall, stopped me from entering. Instead of Gordon's voice I heard Paul—'Wah wah wah wah . . . Bam bam bam . . . the forest . . . the trees . . . little Eva—Orphan Annie . . . Trouble I *don't* like . . .' His maddeningly quick voice drowned out Gordon's voice. I knew that to Paul I was as the life I'd lived. Paul didn't see me as Gordon saw me. 'A pure-hearted girl,' he had said. 'One of the prettiest girls in the world,' he had said. And——

'Oh, my *darling* . . .' he had said.

'Oh *my d*arling,' I whispered, and everything became beautiful and possible again. I put my hand over the place where my buried treasure lay. Tomorrow I must ask Gordon to tell me the meaning of the song imprisoned in the old music-box, imprisoned in the earth beneath my hand.

'You havink a happy dream, Sleena, so I tink.' I heard Mr Faber speaking to me.

I turned my face to where his voice came from, I smiled and said, 'Yes, Mr Faber—a happy and a mighty fine dream.'

CHAPTER TWENTY-THREE

Rose-ann had spent her day in 'Ladies' on her feet. She was hung over. She'd cleaned up after sluts of all kinds all day through.

I felt sorry for Rose-ann.

Nothing in the room was the way Rose-ann wanted it. Nothing.

Everything in the room was a mess.

I'd cleaned and neatened the room but I couldn't see it. Rose-ann could. It about drove her mad.

'You cleaned this room today, Sleena?'

'Yes, yes I did, Rose-ann.'

'I been cleaning up after sluts all day. I got to come home and clean up after the biggest slut of all. You know who—to whom I speak, Sleena?'

'Have I spilt something, Rose-ann? Tell me—I'll fix it.'

Rose-ann wouldn't answer me. She began to make a banging and crashing of pans and cooking things. She sloshed a wet cloth about the room and as she worked her voice became louder and angrier.

'Sluts and sluts, nothing in my life but cleaning up after sluts. Jeez! How I hate sluts—but good. Me cleaning up after sluts.' Rose-ann opened the cupboard where we kept our cooking pans. The pans made hot banging clashes as she swept them on to the floor.

'Oh you *slut.*' Rose-ann sloshed me but good with her wet cleaning cloth. 'Oh you *slut!*' she yelled.

I wished for sure that she would stop saying that word.

'I'm sorry, Rose-ann,' I said. 'I'll neaten up the pans. I'm sorry if they were in a pile. Let me neaten things up.' I had to yell above the noise of the banging kitchen things. Rose-ann yelled back at me. The room was full of our yelling, crashing metal and steamy hot hard-to-breathe air. Ole Pa opened the door and he began to yell louder than anything in the room. He yelled and thumped loud and hard. This went to Rose-ann's head. Rose-ann went wild. The metal pans hit the walls as she threw them. Hit me, hit Ole Pa. Rose-ann never stopped yelling for a second. Her voice became louder with every word she uttered. The words became dirtier.

It was like being in a storm. A bad storm. I became scared. Storms I couldn't take. I crawled beneath my bed and made myself as small as when I was a little girl. I closed my ears with my hands.

Ole Pa had no fear of storms of any kind. He was mad crazy with Rose-ann's goings on. He was, it seemed to me, having himself a ball. Everything that hit him he was sending back to Rose-ann and this made her wilder than ever.

Rose-ann pulled out every drawer and tipped out the things in them. I heard them falling and skittering.

Suddenly Rose-ann missed me. She began to hunt about the room.

'Sleena . . . Sleenah . . .'

I pressed against the wall. I felt Rose-ann's hands catch me. Her hands didn't seem like hands but like searching claws. I knew that she meant to hurt me, to hurt me bad.

I screamed. Rose-ann dragged me out. I fought against her. I tried to keep my face hidden from Rose-ann.

The pain of being dragged out of my hiding-place by my hair hurt in a way I'd never known before. I was filled with crazy anger. I screamed louder and louder.

Ole Pa joined in. I think Ole Pa was trying to pull Rose-ann off me. He was yelling. I was yelling. Rose-ann opened her lungs and yelled louder and bigger than a woman should be able.

I was on the floor under both Rose-ann and Ole Pa. My face was bleeding from the scratches made by the long sharp nails Rose-ann was so all-fired proud of, and I stopped yelling because I'd no breath left in my body. I know Ole Pa meant the mighty kick he gave to land on Rose-ann, but just my luck, it landed in my soft middle. I was trying to draw breath when the door opened and residents came rushing in. The residents were yelling too. They sounded like at a ball game, full of excitement and interest.

I heard Mrs Favaloro because she yelled in her language of Italian, and sounded louder than anyone. The head cheerleader.

Even bleeding and trying to get a breath I felt shame that a woman as respectable as Mrs Favaloro should see us like we were, see me and my family being so very unrespectable. I knew we would never live it down.

I got my breath. I sat on the floor and listened to things untangle. Ole Pa and Rose-ann banded together and pushed and yelled at the residents. I never heard such a brawl—I'd heard some mighty fine sized brawls but none like this one.

Suddenly the room was quiet. Mr and Mrs Favaloro were the last to leave. After what Rose-ann said to Mr Favaloro about his wife I feared that no matter how he trusted her, how faithful and true a wife she had been to him, he couldn't but in the future have a few doubts raised in his mind about her goings on during his time away from their room. Rose-ann knew dreadful things to say about people. Although I knew how decent Mrs Favaloro was I began to wonder—had I missed out on some of her goings on with men.

Mrs Favaloro gave way to screaming tears. Italians can cry much louder than people like us. I never heard such a sound, such rich full crying and talking.

The room became crazy still and quiet, like after a true storm.

I heard Ole Pa rubbing his hands together.

'We fixed 'em,' he said. 'We fixed 'em, Rose-ann, huh!' He sounded happy and like a young man.

'Sure.' Rose-ann was breathing in sharp quick breaths, but she, like Ole Pa, sounded happy and young.

They started to laugh. They laughed like I never heard them laugh before. They laughed so much that they couldn't talk and their bellies hurt them.

'Oh my achin' belly,' gasped Ole Pa.

'Hoo hoo hoo . . . a-hah a-hah-hah. Oh Jeez! Hah hah *hah* . . .' Rose-ann was fit to be tied. They staggered about the room. Couldn't find a place to settle. One would stop for a second, the other would say: 'Did you get a load of . . . ?' Off they'd go again. I began to feel sick. I was sick on the floor, just where I was sitting.

It seemed I'd never stop. I'd never been so sick in my life. Even when there was nothing else in me I went on and on.

CHAPTER TWENTY-FOUR

Rose-ann and Ole Pa had laughed with fresh laughter when I started to be sick. They grew quieter as I went on and on. The only sound in the room was me being sick. It sure sounded bad.

'Stop it. Stop that, Sleena,' said Rose-ann.

'Leave her be. She's sick,' said Ole Pa, and he sounded like an unhappy, very old, old man. 'She sick—Sleena's sick. You sick, Sleena?' he asked me.

'Get up,' said Rose-ann. 'Get up, Sleena, you slut. You sitting in your own sick like a pig. You are a no-good blind pig and a slut to boot. Get up, Sleena.'

'I can't,' I said.

'Leave me help you.' Rose-ann pulled me up by my hair. I never noticed the pain.

'Don't,' said Ole Pa. 'Don't hurt Sleena, Rose-ann.'

'I'll do as I like,' said Rose-ann.

Ole Pa was quiet. I heard him sit on his bed. I heard the big tired sigh he gave. It sounded so empty of everything good in life. I could've cried for Ole Pa.

'What you sitting down for? Sleena'll only spread this vomit if she cleans it. You clean up after Sleena—huh?'

Rose-ann spoke to Ole Pa. I knew by her voice that the laughs they'd shared were over. 'I can't clean up this of Sleena's,' Rose-ann said. 'You like this blind slut. You clean it up.'

'No,' said Ole Pa. 'You clean it up.'

'No.' Rose-ann went to the bathroom and banged the door shut. I heard water running into the tub. She was going to take a bath.

'I feel sick, Ole Pa,' I said. I did, I felt sick for sure.

'Me too,' said Ole Pa. 'I'm an old man, Sleena. Too old. I'm going out to get shikkered, Sleena. I can't clean up. I'd like to but I can't. You understand, Sleena? I can't.'

'Do you have to go, Ole Pa?'

'I have to. I'm sorry, Sleena.'

Ole Pa did sound sorry. It was just that he couldn't help himself. He had to go and get drunk. Ole Pa went out of the room. I listened to his steps on the stairs. I wished he hadn't gone. I wished he hadn't left me alone with Rose-ann. I felt frightened, scared of being alone with Rose-ann. I couldn't forget the hatred I'd felt in her grasping scratching hands as she pulled me from beneath the bed.

Carefully and quietly I took a sheet off my bed and cleaned up the mess I'd made on the floor. A good thing we'd no carpet. I folded the messy sheet as small as possible and stuffed it into the trash can.

I crawled over to the sink. I knew better than to walk. The floor was littered with pans, forks, knives, clothing, odds and ends.

I soaped a cloth and crawled back. I did this three times— it seemed to take for ever. At least I knew that I'd cleaned up what I'd caused.

It was crazy hard picking up the pans and other things, not knowing where they were. Without making a sound I had most of the hard stuff put back in their places. I began to pick up and sort out the clothing. It wasn't so bad because I know the feel of everything we own and I know exactly where they belong. At least things would look better for Rose-ann when she came out.

I had to sit down. I sat on my bed and waited.

I hoped and I prayed that Rose-ann would go out. Hoped that it wasn't still one of her off-nights. If she was going out her mind wouldn't be on me or on the room. I knew there were still things lying about. I just felt unable to do any more.

When I heard the water gurgling down the pipes and smelt the sweet heavy smell of talcum powder I knew that Rose-ann was coming out. I tried to tell myself that the queer tight fear I felt was only because of the rhubarb we'd had, just nerves.

Rose-ann breezed into the room. I heard her grunting as she struggled into her girdle. She didn't speak to me and when, to be polite, I said.

'I've neatened up a bit, Rose-ann.' She didn't answer, just began to hum and sing.

Her voice was husky and deep and she sang as if she was alone in the room.

'See what the boys in the back room'll have
And tell 'em that I'll have the same . . .'

Rose-ann went right on with her song. I felt queer and
really like I wasn't in the room, like she was pretending.

'Rose-ann,' I said, 'are you going out?'

'And tell 'em—
Tell 'em that I'll have the same . . .'

Rose-ann began to put on her face. I knew she was going
out. I took a long deep breath. I was glad for sure that she
was going out. I'd no need to be scared, no need at all. Rose-
ann was just Rose-ann. No different from usual. I took
another long deep breath. I began to feel much better.

'Sleena?' said Rose-ann. Very high tone.

'Yes?' I said.

'Yes whom?'

'Rose-ann,' I said. 'Yes, Rose-ann?'

'That's more like it. Sleena, tell old Faber not to bring no
more beads. Tell him you got a new job.'

I knew I'd not heard right.

'I beg your pardon, Rose-ann,' I said. 'I thought you said to
tell Mr Faber not to bring any more beads for me to thread?'

'That's right.' Rose-ann was doing her mouth.

Not to bring any more beads to thread? I knew I'd not
heard right. I had heard right but I couldn't't've heard right?

'Tell Mr Faber . . .?' I asked stupidly.

'That's right.'

I was ashamed of the thin shaky laugh I gave. The scared
unknown fear was back in me again. I pressed my hands
tightly together.

'What you laughing at, Sleena?' asked Rose-ann, and her
voice was like her voice, but not like it. I felt cold. Suddenly,
although the room was hotter than ever I began to shiver.

'You making with the funny, Rose-ann?' I said, and I was
sorry to hear my cheap little laugh in the room.

'No,' said Rose-ann.

What had got into Rose-ann? A hundred times I'd cried
and asked if I couldn't do other work than thread beads.
Hundreds of times Rose-ann had said I'd do beads—or else.
Now she was saying: no more beads.

'What's got into you, Rose-ann?' I asked. My voice was like my laugh.

'You being cheeky, Sleena?'

'No, oh no, Rose-ann. I'm just surprised that's all.'

'You're going to be more surprised in the near future,' said Rose-ann. 'Me and Sadie, we got plans for you, Sleena.'

'Plans! Plans? You and Sadie?' My head seemed to be floating in the air above my head. I held my head in my hands. I felt I was going to be sick again. I didn't want to be sick again. I pressed my hands against my stomach.

'Me and Sadie,' said Rose-ann.

Even if I'd never known Gordon I knew I could never do the things Rose-ann and Sadie did. If it meant I had to kill myself, I knew that I could never do what they did. I thought back on the night the unknown man had locked Rose-ann out into the hallway. I *remembered*. I began to be sick again.

'Now lay that. Now stop that, Sleena.'

I stopped being sick.

'I can't do what you ask, Rose-ann,' I said, and my voice was deep.

'No one's asking you anything, Sleena,' said Rose-ann. 'I'm *telling* you. Me and Sadie, we got plans. Sadie's smart. Sadie says you can be a pay-off. Sadie says you will be a curiosity, a gas-like-wow! Sadie says it's time I got a reward for the long years I kept you. Sadie says it's time I left "Ladies" and took it easy. Sadie's but smart.' Rose-ann kicked one of the pans I'd left on the floor.

'Sadie is a bad woman,' I said. I'd not meant to knock Sadie to Rose-ann, I couldn't stop the words.

'Sadie's swell. Sadie's a doll, a living doll,' said Rose-ann.

'Ole Pa—Ole Pa won't let you do it. Ole Pa will stop you,' I said.

'Hoo hoo! Old bum! What—I ask you—can he do?'

I knew I should keep quiet. I knew that Rose-ann was only pretending. She had to be only pretending. Rose-ann was my mother. When I'd been little, Rose-ann had read stories to me. Sometimes when I'd been a small girl she'd even held me on her knee. I remembered plain as plain all the nice things Rose-ann had done for me when I'd been a small girl.

'You're a laugh, Rose-ann,' I said.

'Yeah,' she said, 'aren't I?'

I knew that Rose-ann wasn't pretending and I knew she really did hate me. Every little bit of me.

The darkness I lived in became darker. I'd never known such black darkness. It wasn't the thought of the work Rose-ann had planned for me that gave such a sad darkness—it was because she was my mother.

'Oh, Rose-ann,' I whispered.

'That's me.' Rose-ann sounded real chipper. I knew I would never do what she wanted. I'd had a shock. I sat on the bed and got over the shock. I wouldn't say any more to her. I'd let her think I could do nothing but what she wanted. I'd be smarter than Rose-ann—or Sadie.

I lay down on my bed.

'You rehearsing, Sleena?' Rose-ann laughed, and I hated the sound of her laugh.

'I'm tired,' I said. 'I'm most terribly tired.'

'You'll know what it's like to be tireder. I'm off out now, Sleena. Me and Sadie, we got to see a gent. We got a swell apartment in view, me and Sadie.'

I sat up and put my feet on the floor.

'What do you mean?' I asked.

'What do you mean—who?'

'Rose-ann. What do you mean, Rose-ann?'

'That's better. I mean me and Sadie—we're moving in together. Me an' Sadie an' you, Sleena. That Sadie! She's but smart.'

'And—Ole Pa?'

'Never you mind about Ole Pa,' said Rose-ann.

Rose-ann sounded like Ole Pa was dead and buried. I didn't like the way she spoke about Ole Pa. A sort of secret *knowing*.

'What do you mean, Rose-ann?'

I heard her open the door. Before she went out, Rose-ann said, 'Ole Pa! He's going to die soon is Ole Pa. That's what I mean about Ole Pa, Sleena.'

Ole Pa going to die? It wasn't true. Ole Pa was old but he was strong, strong and healthy.

'You are telling a lie,' I said. I knew she was lying.

Rose-ann laughed. 'If you wasn't blind, Sleena—if you could see and had brains to read, I'd show you, let you read the letter I have about Ole Pa.'

'Letter? About Ole Pa? You have no letter. You never get letters.'

'I got this letter. This letter I got from the doctor.'

She wasn't lying. 'Which doctor?' I asked. 'Ole Pa's never been to a doctor in his life.'

'Hoo hoo! Smarty pants! The doctor where me and Ole Pa works—that doctor. We have check-ups. That's what we have, Miss Smarty Pants. Ole Pa has a cancer. A bad cancer. Ole Pa don't know it but he'll be dead and buried before Fall. That's what!' Rose-ann sounded happy for sure. Sounded like she was glad her father had a bad cancer and would be dead and buried. Ole Pa! Dying!

'Does Ole Pa know?' I asked.

'Who you talking to?'

'To you,' I said.

'Then have manners, use my name.'

'Does Ole Pa know he's sick . . . Rose-ann?'

'He does not. The doc called me in. Next of kin I am. The doc said the old man don't know anything, thinks he's in a swell condition. How you like that for a laugh? The doc give me a shot of brandy after he told me. That was a laugh. "No need to upset the old man," he said. "Let the old man just go on a while." He'd know soon enough, the doc said. Man! That doc is quite a guy. Big, attractive—know what I mean? Huh?' Rose-ann made sloppy kissing noises.

I knew what she meant. Maybe Rose-ann hated me but the way she hated me was but nothing to the way I felt about Rose-ann.

'What did he mean—Ole Pa would know soon enough?' I added, 'Rose Ann.'

'The cancer's going to start biting into him. Right into his guts. That's how. Now you hush up. I'm going out. I got big things on my mind. I got a big deal.'

I heard the tip tap tip of high heels running heavily down the stairs. Then I heard them running up the stairs again. Rose-ann opened the door and yelled at me.

'One thing more I meant to say to you. You play up—you just play up about one little thing even—you do that and I push this news of Ole Pa right into his mouth. I'll see he *eats* this letter—after I've read it to him. You know what I mean, Sleena?'

'Don't you care about Ole Pa? Don't you even care one little bit about Ole Pa, Rose-ann?' I asked slowly.

'That's a laugh,' said Rose-ann.

I heard the tip tap tip of her heels once more. This time they didn't come back.

I sat on the bed and I thought about Ole Pa. I never thought about Sadie or about what she and Rose-ann were making plans for. I never thought about Gordon. I could only think about poor old Ole Pa.

'I brung you some ice-cream, Sleena.'

'What flavour, Ole Pa?'

'Guess? You have to guess, Sleena . . .'

Ole Pa had been in my life ever since I'd been born. Ole Pa'd taken care of me more than anyone in the world.

In all my life Ole Pa'd never hit me. He'd thumped and shouted at me. Been mean as dirt to me time and again, but he'd never hit me apart from paddling me, times I deserved it.

'I'm a flop, Sleena, an old no good drunk an' a f-l-o-p flop.' Time and again I'd heard him say those words and listened to his old man's yawn.

I couldn't bear that Ole Pa was going to have a cancer biting into him. I loved Ole Pa. I knew that I loved him and I wanted to punish myself that I'd not known before this that I loved him.

'I love you, Ole Pa,' I cried. 'I love you—but good . . .'

I cried and cried. I couldn't stop my crying for Ole Pa who was going to be dead before the Fall came.

I took the sheets off his bed. He wasn't due for clean sheets until Sunday. I couldn't think what I could do for him, except for giving him clean fresh sheets before they were due.

I waited and waited for him to come home. When he came home he was so shikkered he couldn't make it to the bed, just lay on the floor. I tried to shift him, but he was too heavy. I took out his dentures and put them to float in his glass. Once he'd nearly taken his death from them going down his throat a ways.

I sat beside him on the floor and I wondered, would I've done better to leave them in, let them choke him before the cancer started biting at him? I didn't know. I didn't know anything much at all. I lay beside Ole Pa and fell asleep holding his horny old hand in mine. Man! I sure knew I loved him.

CHAPTER TWENTY-FIVE

Ole Pa woke up during the night and spoke very rudely to me. He got into his bed and I got into mine. I felt strange! I felt better after I took my shoes off and got back into bed with the rest of my clothes on. I was but tired. In the morning the smell of coffee perking woke me up. Rose-ann was already dressed and had her face on even. It had been a long time since Rose-ann had made the morning coffee.

I lay in bed and listened to her. She was singing. Rose-ann was feeling mighty spry and happy. It was fine lying in bed smelling coffee and listening to someone singing. Then in a flash I remembered.

I remembered the rhubarb from the night before. I felt the rough scratches on my face. My body was aching. I remembered the plans Rose-ann was making with Sadie. I remembered about Ole Pa.

I sat up.

'Good morning good morning good morning.' Rose-ann, I thought, was over-acting. No one could feel as grand as she sounded after all we'd been through the night before.

'Good morning, Rose-ann,' I said in my deep voice.

'Rise an' shine. Upsey daisy. Toodle-oo an' pip pip,' yelled Rose-ann. 'Up an' on with it, Sleena.'

I got out of bed.

'What you sleep with your clothes on for?' Rose-ann was surprised.

'I was too tired to get undressed, Rose-ann.'

'Take a bath. You look like a mess, Sleena. This whole place looks like a mess. Man! I'm hep today. Man! Sleena, me an' Sadie seen our new place last night. Like—*wow!* You wait you see our new place, Sleena.'

'I'll never see it,' I said. I'd hoped I'd been dreaming up that part of last night.

'What's that?' The bright tone went out of her. I heard the threat in her voice. What had she said? 'You play up an' Ole

104

Pa'll eat the doc's letter . . .' I was ashamed of my thin laugh.

'A blind tomato like me won't ever see nothing, Rose-ann. That's what I mean,' I said.

Rose-ann was silent like she was thinking things over.

'Oh *that*,' she said.

'Yeah, that.'

'Man!' said Rose-ann. 'I never in all my life seen a sweller place. That Sadie, she's smart! You should've heard Sadie dickering over the rental, Sleena. I was fit to be tied. Sadie's smart.'

'I'll bet,' I said.

Rose-ann was quiet again.

'You being cheeky, Sleena?' she asked.

'No,' I said.

'Hmmm! That's good. You should've heard Sadie, Sleena, no kidding.' Rose-ann just couldn't get over the smartness of Sadie. I'd never known her so happy.

'Did she get the apartment? Is it all settled, Rose-ann?'

'Never you mind about that, Sleena. You just do as you're told. Sadie and me's running things.' Her voice was proud. She came over to the bed and the sound of her low, 'between you and me' voice made me feel dirty.

'Sleena,' she said. 'You tell old Faber to bring one week's more beads for you to do. Sadie says, no need to throw good money away. Sadie says in a week she can work the rental down.'

'How?' I asked. 'Why can she work the rental down on such a swell place? What's wrong with the place?'

I felt her breath on my cheek. I wanted to lean away from Rose-ann but I knew better.

'Sadie says on account of the area—on account of the apartment being in a coloured area and on account of us being white.' Rose-ann drew in her breath with pride at Sadie's smartness.

Come what may I knew I'd never live with Rose-ann and Sadie in their new apartment, but like the rats were after my thoughts I seemed to hear the voices of black men waiting to get into the swell apartment, waiting to get at me.

I put my hands over my face and bent forward.

'What you doing that for?' Rose-ann asked.

I uncovered my face. 'Tell me more about Sadie,' I said.

'That Sadie! Oh that Sadie! She slays me. I could've died, Sleena, no kidding.'

I wished you had, I thought. I wished you had died, you and your doll of a Sadie both.

'Tell me,' I asked. 'Tell me what you aim to do about Ole Pa. Ole Pa going to move in with us until . . . ?'

'He is not,' Rose-ann was very high tone.

'You got plans for Ole Pa, Rose-ann?'

Rose-ann stood up. 'He stays here. Pains get bad and he stops going to 'Mens,' then Sadie says he goes to the Clinic. Smart? That's what she is. See! Into the Clinic—all over! No trouble to no one.'

'Oh!' I said.

'What you mean, "Oh"?' asked Rose-ann, and I knew by her voice that she was not happy. Not really happy about going in with Sadie, and letting Ole Pa die of a cancer on his own, in a clinic.

Now that I thought about it, for years I'd listened to Sadie and Rose-ann talking on their Sundays together. I'd heard them talking but never listened to the meaning of their words. Now I remembered that Sadie had never let up on wanting Rose-ann to 'join forces' with her.

Sadie was stronger than Rose-ann. Rose-ann was frightened of Sadie because she was weaker than her. I remembered all the talks I'd heard and I knew that Rose-ann was trapped by Sadie's strength. She didn't want to live and work with Sadie but she'd never be brave enough to tell Sadie so. I felt sorry for Rose-ann. I hated her for sure, but I felt sorry for her too.

'Rose-ann,' I whispered. 'I meant, couldn't all this, about the new place and all, couldn't it wait till after—you know till when! Till after—Fall?'

'Sadie says, we let this chance pass we never get another chance. Sadie says time I had a break. Sadie's right. I'm due for a break. Years I never had a break. Years I cleaned up after sluts . . .'

If Rose-ann started up again about sluts I knew that even if it woke Ole Pa I'd start yelling. I couldn't listen any more to Rose-ann. Everything she was saying was nothing to do with me. Could never be anything to do with me. I sat up straight and I took a deep breath.

I *was* going to have a new kind of life. I was going to learn to read and write. What would Rose-ann say if I told her:

'Rose-ann, you and Sadie go ahead with your plans—go right ahead. But count me out of yours and Sadie's plans, Rose-ann, I got plans for myself.'

'What plans pray?' Rose-ann would ask, very high tone.

'Oh,' and I would answer also high tone. 'Oh, I'm thinking of writing a book, Rose-ann . . .'

Man! That would slay her for sure. I giggled.

'You gone mad or something?' asked Rose-ann.

'No,' I said. 'No, Rose-ann. Could I have a cup of Java before I have my bath, Rose-ann? Shall I make something for you to eat, Rose-ann?' (I hate you Rose-ann, I thought, I hate you.)

'You look a mess, Sleena. You take a bath. Ole Pa! Ole Pa's got to wake up. Time he got up.' Rose-ann yelled into Ole Pa's ear: 'You never waking up today? You retired or something?'

Ole Pa sat up. He was mad at Rose-ann for yelling at him. He couldn't stand to be yelled at in the morning. Ole Pa socked Rose-ann. I held my breath, hoping Rose-ann, knowing Ole Pa had a cancer and would be dead come Fall, wouldn't hit back at him. She didn't.

'You old bum,' she said. 'You sock me again, you be sorry you sock me again, you old bum.'

Rose-ann laughed and Ole Pa let fly with some very dirty words. All my life, every day of my life I'd heard dirty words. I'd never noticed them, just they were part of people. Nowadays I noticed them and I didn't like hearing them.

To stop Ole Pa's swearing and dirt, I yelled out:

'Ole Pa! Good morning, Ole Pa.'

This made him madder than ever.

'Quit yellin'. Quit yelling at me, you blind tart. I live with two tarts. Which is worse of you both I don't know. I live in a dirty mess of tarts.' Ole Pa thumped and yelled. I hoped Rose-ann wouldn't take him up on it and she didn't. If I'd had a hope it wasn't true that Ole Pa had a cancer—I knew now that he had one for sure. I knew that Rose-ann would never behave so gentle if Ole Pa wasn't going to die soon.

'Hush up, Ole Pa, here's a cup of coffee,' said Rose-ann to Ole Pa.

Like me, Ole Pa was surprised. He scratched his head.

'What's got into you, Rose-ann?' he asked. He sounded uneasy, suspicious. I would have been too, if I'd not known the facts of the case.

'Hoo hoo!" said Rose-ann, 'I just come into a million bucks. I just got myself married to a millionaire. I just feel mighty good today. I just love everyone today. That's what's got into me. Hoo hoo!'

Ole Pa stumped to the bathroom. Before he closed the door on himself he yelled:

'Up both of you.'

Rose-ann laughed like it was spring and the daffodils were out in the park.

'Old bum,' she laughed, 'finished old bum.'

Rose-ann said good-bye to me. Her steps on the stairs sounded crisp and young.

I was glad she had gone. I had so many things to think about, to sort out. So many new, difficult and ugly things to sort out.

I waited for Ole Pa to finish with the bathroom.

I wanted to be kind and gentle to Ole Pa but it was a waste trying. He was hung over for sure.

I remembered to be tolerant. I did all I could to be tolerant with Ole Pa but the demons were in him.

'Here's your coffee, Ole Pa,' I said.

'Sleena,' said Ole Pa, 'I wouldn't touch no coffee given to me by a mess such as you are. Sleena, you look a bigger lush than your two bucks a time mother.' Ole Pa thumped on the table. I jumped.

'I'm a mess I know,' I said.

'No,' said Ole Pa. 'You couldn't know. You couldn't know what a mess you look, Sleena. God help me, I got eyes. You got no eyes, Sleena. Your Pa cut up your Ma's man and your two-bit mother, she threw acid and burnt out your eyes. Nice eyes you had too—big lovely clear blue eyes you had. You ain't got no eyes at all now, Sleena. No eyes at all, an' you're but a mess.'

Ole Pa told me all this like I was hearing it for the very first time. He wanted to me to feel as low and bad as he did.

'I know,' I said. 'I know all that, Ole Pa. I know I'm blind, and I know I look a mess. I'm sorry about that, Ole Pa. Won't you have your drink of coffee? It sure smells good.'

'Hand me my dentures.' Ole Pa had taken his dentures from me every morning since for ever.

I handed him his dentures and he went to the bathroom to clean them.

He wouldn't say good-bye to me. I heard his steps stumping slowly down the stairs.

I began to worry about what was going to become of Ole Pa after he died. Just like I know about God, I know about Hell.

Unless a miracle happened, I knew for sure that Ole Pa was heading in a very hot direction. I didn't want that he would have to live for ever in a lake of fire.

I knelt down and asked God that He would let a miracle happen—a miracle that would take care of Ole Pa's future.

It sure would have to be some miracle.

When I'd finished my long prayer, I felt a bit easier, not much, but a bit. It was such a short time—until the Fall . . .

I knelt down again and told God that Ole Pa only had until the Fall. I felt a bit crazy telling God who knows everything about that, but I was nervous. I didn't want to take any chances.

Mr Faber was coming to take me to Park. I'd have to hustle. It seemed so long, years and years since yesterday.

I lay in the tub and felt slowly better and better.

I thought how dreadful my future, my life would be if I'd never gone to Park. Never met Gordon.

If I'd never met Gordon, I would have had to kill myself, for sure. I would be lying in my bath wondering how to kill myself.

Instead of that, I was wondering and planning how to tell Gordon that we'd have to hurry, hurry like crazy, about his plans for me and my future.

'Oh—my—darling,' I said, and I put my head under the water and heard the funny strange sounds we hear when we put our heads under the bath water.

CHAPTER TWENTY-SIX

I felt two-faced letting Mr Faber carry the seven bead boxes and my rug all the way to Park.

After his kindness of yesterday, I couldn't tell him that not for anything could I work at beads today—not for anything!

'You vill vork good, Sleena, yes?' Mr Faber sounded uneasy, maybe he felt something different about me?

'Yes. Yes I will work hard, Mr Faber,' I lied. It was a bad feeling lying to Mr Faber.

'You are my bust vorker, Sleena.' Mr. Faber had pride in his voice—for me. I felt bad for sure.

I sat once again beneath my tree. I waited for Gordon and as I waited I listened to the people about me.

The heat of the day was sending many people to the Park. I'd never heard so many people. I was nervous when two women came and sat under my tree. Did they have to sit under my tree? Surely there were other places to sit? I wished for sure that Gordon would hurry, that we would leave Park and go to his apartment, and be alone.

I had so much to tell him. Where would I begin to tell Gordon of the lifetime I'd lived through since yesterday at five o'clock?

I couldn't make up my mind. I let myself drift. I knew that once he came, when we were alone, everything would flow out easily, with no shame and no fear.

I loved him. I loved Gordon with all my heart. I wanted to have a bigger heart so that my love would be bigger, finer and better. I sat and willed my heart to grow bigger. I think it did a little, but not enough—my love flowed over the edges.

I remembered something I'd heard once. I didn't know where it came from, but the time I'd heard it I'd shivered with happiness. I sat under the tree and whispered the words I remembered and didn't know where they came from, over and over.

'Until my cup runneth over. Until my cup runneth over.' It was hotter than almost I could bear under the tree, but once again the words made me shiver with a happiness I couldn't understand. I must ask Gordon who said those words. He'd know.

The far-away clock struck eleven times. The two women still shared the breathless shade of my tree. They talked and talked. They took no notice of me. Not the slightest. I felt queer. At first I'd not heard what they were talking about but as time went by I listened with interest. They were very nice people, they talked about their children. Man! I was surprised. They loved their children—no doubt about that.

I became so deep in their talk that it was hard not to join in. When I heard how Tim, one of the boys of one of them, after all his years of fine school grades was slacking off, his mother was worried about Tim, fit to be tied about his slacking off; I was worried too.

'Is it girls?' the other mother asked.

'Girls? Well of course that accounts for a bit of it, but Tim's always been popular with girls, you know that, Mary. Your own Patty's . . .'

'Patty's always had a crush on Tim.'

'It's not girls. It's a kind of restlessness. I can't quite put my finger on it. Dad and I are fit to be tied about Tim . . .'

Tim's mother was upset about Tim. I longed to know what it was that caused his restlessness but they changed the subject. This happened all the time. Just as I became madly interested they'd change the subject.

'Fingers! Talking about fingers, honey,' one of the mothers laughed (not Tim's mother). 'Janie came to breakfast this morning with her nails dripping scarlet. You know what Harold is like about his Janie . . .'

'He thinks the sun gets up to make that child warm.'

'He does. He spoils her. But could you help it—so cute, so darling . . .'

'She is a honey. Go on, what did Harold do?'

'He ordered her to remove it. Said if she had to paint her pretty nails, for Pete's sake do it in a softer colour.' Janie's mother laughed. So did Tim's.

'Did she?'

'She went off dripping scarlet.'

The mothers laughed at Janie and the father who loved and spoiled her. I wanted to laugh with them. I sure wished Harry had been like Janie's father.

I thought of Rose-ann and her plans for her daughter. I wondered what these mothers would think if they knew what kind of mother I had. Would they be sad for me? Would they stand up and go running from under the tree? I didn't know.

A while back I'd felt my heart beat faster. Among the footsteps on the path I'd 've taken a long shot that I'd heard Gordon walking. I'd been wrong. What was holding him up? Why didn't he come?

The two mothers suddenly made up their minds to have hair-do's. Just like that!

Off they went. Out of my life. No sooner had they gone than Gordon came and sat beside me.

I'd never heard him walking along the path. No one had walked along the path for quite a while. I knew he'd been near by for some time. I was so glad to be near him I never asked him. My cup of happiness overflowed for sure.

Without a word I put out my hand and Gordon held it. We sat for a long time like that.

'What has happened to your face, Selina?' Gordon asked me about the marks on my face.

Now! I would tell him, tell him everything. I tried to tell him but my throat hurt and I couldn't get a word out.

I moved my lips but no sound came from them.

'Has something—something unpleasant happened, Selina?'

Unpleasant! With no warning I began to weep, like a storm was in me.

'Don't,' said Gordon. 'Don't do that Selina. Not here. Not here in the park, honey.' He sounded upset because I was crying in the Park. Perhaps people never cried in the Park. I didn't know.

'I can't stop, just like that,' I cried. 'How can I?'

'You can. You can stop just like—that,' Gordon said. 'I know you can. Do it for me, darling. Stop crying.'

I stopped crying.

'My *brave* baby.' Gordon was proud of me. I laughed because he was pleased with me. Not much of a laugh, but I laughed.

'Now!' Gordon lit a cigarette and threw it away after one puff. He took my hands and I was on my feet the way I loved. No effort of mine.

'Are we going to your place?' I asked.

'Yes.' Gordon sounded undecided. His voice brightened as he said: 'Yes, to my place. Selina, I wanted to talk to you. Talk to you here in the park before going home. I want to talk to you very much.'

'Can't we talk at your place?'

'We can, certainly we can. I wanted to talk to you specially. You see, Paul is at home and I wanted to talk to you alone.'

I was glad he wanted to talk to me alone.

'Then, talk to me,' I said. I sat down on the grass again. 'Let's talk,' I said.

'No, we'll talk about my problem another time.'

'Problem? Do you have problems too?' I was surprised for sure. I sounded surprised.

'Every man born of woman has problems,' he said.

'Tell me yours,' I begged. I wanted to know everything about him.

'No,' said Gordon. 'My problem can wait. Come on, Selina.' Once again I was on my feet. 'I want to know what has happened in your life since yesterday.'

He picked up my boxes and rug.

'Selina,' said Gordon, 'let's go home.'

This time I loved the ride in the elevator. It felt fine.

'I loved that,' I said. 'Gordon, could we go down and up again, once more? Could we?'

'Hold tight.' Gordon started the elevator and we went to the top floor and zooom . . . down again. I loved it.

'Do they have elevators that need folk to drive them full time?' I asked.

'Certainly. You thinking of applying for position of elevator operator, Miss D'arcey?' Gordon was teasing me. I didn't mind.

'Could I?' I asked. Surely I couldn't. Could I?

'You could,' said Gordon. 'But this is no time or place to talk about it. Hear that buzzer? Someone else wants the elevator.'

'Man! Let's get out. We don't want trouble with the residents.' I remembered last night and the trouble at our place. 'Let's hurry,' I said.

'Wait for me,' laughed Gordon. I waited for him. Paul was talking on the telephone when we first went in to the special clean coolness of the apartment. I thought he was speaking in a foreign language, but he wasn't, he talked English, but so fast it sounded foreign; he never drew breath.

'I know all that—I know that—I understand—I'll take care of it—I know all that—thanks for calling—'bye now.'

Paul clashed the phone down and without change of voice spoke to me. I stuck my head forward and listened like mad to his quick talk.

'So here you are—I never expected to see you again—nice to see you, Selina—glad to see you. Hot isn't it? I ask you—is it hot outside? Man! I dislike the heat. Heat is strictly for cotton pickers. I dislike the heat. Do you dislike heat,

Selina? I see you do. You look played out. Gordon, why do you keep Selina standing? He has vile manners doesn't he, Selina! Sit down. Here, sit here . . .'

Paul led me to a seat. I was glad to sit down. I gave a little bounce—just a little one. Was I really back at Gordon's place again? I was. I drew a long cool breath.

'Hullo, Paul,' I said politely.

Paul laughed. He had a wonderful laugh.

'You sound very gay when you laugh,' I said.

'Lord! Do I sound gay? That means I must be unutterably miserable and sad. I only sound gay when I'm sad. When I'm happy I'm sombre, with the glory of being happy.'

'Make us some coffee, Paul,' said Gordon. He sounded tired, much older than his brother.

'You make it, Daddy-o,' said Paul. 'I want to talk to Selina. You make Selina and me some coffee.'

'No, you make it.'

'Selfish! You can see how selfish he is Selina. He is selfish. He found you—he keeps you. Finders, keepers—losers, weepers. That's my brother's policy.' Paul pretended to weep as he went to make the coffee.

'Excuse me a moment, Selina,' said Gordon, and he followed Paul to the kitchen.

Owing to the fact that I'm blind I can't see. Owing to the fact that I'm blind I can hear much clearer than seeing folk. I curled up on the smooth settee and heard the brothers talking. I loved to hear them talking, Gordon and his brother.

Gordon's voice, so much lower than Paul's, I couldn't hear very well, but I heard Paul's every word.

'Have you got rocks in your head? Bringing that girl here again?'

I was unable to hear Gordon's reply but it made Paul angry. 'Man! You *have* got rocks in your head. Gordon, I'm not knocking you, your whatever it is with this girl, but I've a feeling of trouble about to brew. I have an *inherited* feeling —you know I've always had these premonitions . . .'

The low boom of Gordon's voice broke into his brother's speech. I strained my ears. I heard only Paul's reply.

'You've always had a yen to play the harp. I can't imagine how you let yourself become involved with a business like this. A blind girl to boot! Gordon, I think she comes from a trash heap. I'm scared of trash, dad! Trash—I don't like! Go near it and the stink gets on you, clings to you. From you I learned that lesson. *Hang your harp up, man.* Tell this—tell Selina—tell her anything—tell her you have to leave town in a hurry. Let me tell her . . .'

Oh why wasn't I able to hear what Gordon was saying?

I didn't like the sound of Paul's laugh. He opened the door. I heard Gordon say quietly: 'Close the door, Paul.'

I heard the click as he closed it and another click as he let it open again.

'We've never been each other's keepers, Paul. We've always lived and let live.'

'I don't want to be your keeper, man. I just don't know you. This is not like you. Let the girl know the truth. Know that no matter what, she can never mean anything to you or you to her . . .'

'You said that, Doctor, not me,' Gordon said.

'What the devil do you mean? Do you mean you're going to keep up this farce? It's pathetic. This girl is pathetic. If she could see, if she had her sight, she'd see how things are. She'd know she didn't fit in. She'd be scared. She's a simple little thing. Brought up in a dark hole on a dark street in the city.' Paul stopped talking.

'Her entire life has been just that—dark! We agreed that you aren't my keeper. How about letting me manage things my way. How about that, huh?'

'But goddam! This is not your way. You, with your ethics, times are I've had a belly full of your strict code. I don't dig you. Your gospel has always been truth at all costs, facts are facts, no greys in your gospel, just white and black. No half truths. A lie is a lie. Man! Me! I don't like it.'

'Then keep out of it. Keep out of it, boy. For Pete's sake mind your business. Let me mind mine.'

'I don't think you know what you could be letting us in for. You pick this broken lily—this gal up in the park and bring her to our home. That's not so bad. Bad enough but not so bad. You know who this gal's guardians are, dad? Do her folk know she comes here with you? I see they don't. You're asking for trouble.'

'Maybe I am.' Gordon sounded fed up with Paul. 'Maybe I am at that. I think I can take the consequences. I don't want Selina upset. I'm not having her upset.'

I was that proud. Gordon didn't want me upset. I heard Paul say.

'You make me *sick* man. You make me *cry*. You tell that girl you're leaving town—get shot of her. You tell her or I tell her.'

'You've made a bum pot of coffee there, Paul,' said Gordon. 'You pack up, boy. You say good-bye and you go and play hospitals. I'm making fresh coffee.' He laughed. Not a happy laugh. But he laughed.

'Make a rope while you're about it,' said Paul. 'Make a rope to fit about your neck. You're *nuts*.'

Paul came into the room. He knew I'd heard through the partly open door. He came close to me. I drew back the way I draw back when Rose-ann is about to hit me.

Paul didn't hit me but he said in his quick way.

'I don't suppose I'll be seeing you again, Selina. Has Gordon told you—he just told me—I'm always the last one he tells anything to so I presume he's told you. Too bad, isn't it! I'm going to miss him. All his friends will miss him. Man, how I'm going to miss him.'

Paul was hitting at me. All my life I'd been hit out at. Sadie and Rose-ann had hardened me at being hit out at. I smiled at Paul and said:

'Maybe he will write to us.'

'Write to us?' I'd knocked him for sure.

'Yes,' I said, 'from out of town.' I laughed at Paul as though I was his mother and I was playing games with him.

'Hmmm! Yes,' said Paul. Then he bent towards me. This time I didn't want to back away. (Paul didn't hate me.) 'Hmmm!' he said, and I felt his lips brush my cheek.

'Good-bye, white sugar,' he said. 'You're sweet.'

I put my hand to where he had kissed me and heard him yell to Gordon. 'I'm going, dad. Wam bam! I'm off.'

He banged the door noisily shut. He had gone. Thank God he had gone. I forgot he'd ever been with us; Gordon and I were alone.

'*Gordon*,' I called.

'Coming, Selina.' Gordon brought the coffee. It was hot and fresh.

CHAPTER TWENTY-SEVEN

We sat side by side on the bouncy seat. I felt that I'd just been born. Nothing had ever happened in the world before. This, sitting with Gordon, drinking hot coffee in the air-cooled room seemed like the beginning of life and I smiled at him.

'Are you smiling back at me?' I asked.

'Right back at you,' said Gordon.

'I'm loving you,' I said. 'Are you loving me?'

'I am,' he said.

'How can you love a mess like me?'

'How can I not?' Gordon took my empty cup and he told me I was not a mess.

'You are not a mess. You are beautiful. You are not only beautiful, you are brave and beautiful. I saw a lot of brave soldiers in Korea. I never saw a braver one than a blind girl sitting under an oak tree in a park.'

'Me?'

'In a park. You. Holding a leaf in your hands as though it were a treasure without price. I never saw a braver tightening of lips against pain than the tightening of your lips when the beads rolled down the slope.'

'Oh no.'

'I loved you before I spoke to you. If I'd never spoken to you, I'd never have forgotten you. Never stopped loving you. Yes, I'm loving you.'

'I'm glad. Oh I'm glad you love me,' I whispered, but I was wondering why loving me filled his voice with the pain like toothache. I wanted to take the pain out of his voice.

'But you *did* speak to me,' I said, 'and here we are.'

'Yes.'

'With problems and troubles,' I said.

'Uh-huh.'

'Just now,' I said, 'I have only one problem. It's about killing me. Only you can solve it.'

'I?'

'You.'

'What is it, Selina?'

'I have to be kissed.' It was true. I had to be kissed. Right then. I had to be.

Gordon laughed. He sounded relieved, almost happy.

'You are too young,' he laughed.

'Maybe you are too old,' I said. 'Paul kissed me, he didn't think I was too young. Paul kissed me.'

'He did?' Gordon didn't believe me.

'He did. And he called me white sugar and he said I was sweet!'

'How about that!' said Gordon. 'How *'bout* that!' He sounded really happy. 'Paul's all right,' he said proudly.

'Forget about Paul. Think about me. Think about me, Gordon. Let us have one little monent to be happy in,' I begged. I really begged like a beggar. I wanted so much for Gordon to kiss me. Not a stormy kiss. Not a friendly laughing kiss on my nose or my cheek. I wanted a kiss of love on my mouth that seemed to be burning, on fire. My mouth was on fire, I'd never known such a crazy feeling.

'Please,' I said, and I didn't know my own voice. My voice sounded hot, like my lips.

'No,' said Gordon, and he moved to stand up. I reached out my hand and caught at him. Gordon loosened my hands and moved away. I followed him and we stood together in the room.

'Please . . .' I put my hands against him, against his chest and I felt the thumping of Gordon's heart. It throbbed and thumped, I pressed my hand against it and tried to stop it. I didn't really want it to stop but I knew it was hurting him and I couldn't bear that he get hurt.

'Your heart is hurting you,' I said, and again I didn't know my own voice.

'Yes,' said Gordon and his voice I didn't know. I felt suddenly that he was a stranger to me and I moved quickly away.

'Selina,' Gordon called my name and caught me in his arms. He seemed to know I'd felt him to be a stranger and he held me against him. His hands moved down my arms—over my shoulders—they touched my breasts and burnt through my blouse. His hands were on fire. Everywhere his hands touched me I turned to fire, and when he said my name

again he didn't finish the word for his mouth was on mine
and the air-cooled room became a blazing fire.

Now I knew what it was to love.

'This is love,' I said.

'Yes,' said Gordon and his mouth came down on my
willing mouth. My tongue moved over the smoothness of his
teeth. I loved the smoothness of his teeth and the feel of his
tongue in my mouth. I loved Gordon and kissing, just kissing
and being kissed was not enough. Gordon knew it was not
enough. He carried me through the burning air and we lay
together on his bed.

'You are going to make love with me,' I cried out softly.
I'd never been so mad. Mad and happy.

'Yes.'

Suddenly, unwillingly, I remembered Rose-ann's friend.
Remembered the night he'd locked her into the hall and
what he'd done to me. I wanted to kill Rose-ann and her
friend for doing that to me. With all my heart I wanted
Gordon, who loved me, to be the only man ever to love me.
I couldn't stand remembering that night and as I reached out
to Gordon I said: 'I wish—I wish I'd never been done over
before.' I did. I wished it with all my heart. I reached out for
Gordon and I couldn't find him. He had got off the bed and
was standing beside it.

'What did you say?' he asked.

I was ashamed. I was crazy ashamed. I pressed deeper into
the bed.

'Nothing.'

'*What* did you say?' asked Gordon as though he was asking
me for the first time instead of the second.

'Nothing,' I said.

I heard Gordon leave the room and I heard him taking a
shower. Although I'd no way of knowing, I knew that he
was taking a cold water shower—cold water to take away
the burning that had been in his flesh. It seemed to me that
he was washing away the touch of me—Sleena! Rose-ann's
daughter.

I turned and lay on my stomach and I cried bitterly about
everything. Most of all I cried for Rose-ann's daughter,
Sleena.

If I hadn't been blind I'd have got off that bed and crept
out of Gordon's home. I'd have gone down in the elevator

back to the park. Then I remembered if I'd not been blind I wouldn't have to sit in a park and thread beads. If I'd been able to see I wouldn't have been laid by Rose-ann's friend. If I could see, my life would be so different. I hated being blind. I hated it.

I put my feet to the floor, sat on the edge of the bed and wished I never had to let Gordon see me again.

He saw me again and I'm glad that he did.

I smelt the fresh soap smell I'd smelt before and this time it didn't make my stomach turn over. It made me feel dirty. Gordon sat beside me on his bed and held me against his cool body. All at once my feeling against myself changed. For he held me the way I'd held my oak leaf. How had Gordon said I'd held it? Like it was a treasure beyond price! That's the way he held me and he said:

'I'm sorry, baby.' It was wonderful to have him call me baby. Clean and grand. 'You are my much sinned against baby.'

Gordon made comforting sounds as he stroked my hair with a steady hand.

'I thought you were angry with me,' I said. 'That you thought me to be bad, dirty.' I pressed against his shoulder.

'I know. I know that's what you thought. You were wrong. I had no time to tell you how mistaken you were. Do you understand?'

'Yes,' I said, and I did understand.

'I said what I did because I love you so much,' I told him.

'I know. I know why you said it. Thank God you did. You brought me back to earth—wam! Man, but it hurt, coming back to earth—wam! Just like that!'

I didn't want to laugh but I laughed. Gordon wanted me to laugh.

'I'm glad it hurt you,' I said. And I was glad.

'I want to say: "I forgive you, Gordon."'

'I can't say that. It would be untrue,' I said.

'Then you don't forgive me?'

'I can't. I can't forgive what never happened. I want you to love me. You did nothing.'

'My *pure*-hearted girl,' said Gordon, and the way he said it made me laugh until I cried. All at once I became a grown-up person. It was grand to sit on the bed with Gordon and laugh with him about sex. It was grand.

'It's not funny,' said Gordon and I knew he was grinning. I grinned back at him.

'Isn't it?' I said and we began to laugh again.

'I'm hungry, Gordon, I'm terribly hungry.'

'Me too. Let's eat.' We went into the kitchen together. We ate a fine lunch together in the kitchen. It was fine because we seemed even closer and dearer to each other, not only seemed! We were.

Man, but I loved Gordon.

CHAPTER TWENTY-EIGHT

Loving each other, being together and having such a fine time had pushed all other things out of our minds. When Gordon said, 'Come on, darling. It's getting late,' I didn't want to talk about the bad side of life. I wanted to stay for ever in the clean happy land of Selina.

'Let's leave it till tomorrow,' I said.

'Let's talk now. I have to know about those marks on your face. I have to know why you were so upset in the park this morning. After I know—after that—I'm going to tell you about my problem. You remember I have a problem?'

'Yes,' I said. 'I know I'm your problem.'

'Why should you think that?'

I knew he didn't know I'd overheard him—or rather heard his boom boom boom and Paul's talk. I didn't want ever to keep the truth about anything from Gordon.

'I heard you and Paul in the kitchen. I have amazing ears. To make up for my eyes, you know . . .'

'Do you now? Thank you for telling me. Forewarned—forearmed. You are wrong though. I am *your* problem.'

'In what way? You could never be a problem. Not to me. Paul thinks—and he's right—that I'm not good enough for you. I'm not. I know I'm not. I just love you.'

'Sit down. Sit here. Sit close beside me. Tell me what took place last night. Paul's thoughts are not important.'

Last night? What had taken place last night? I'd forgotten.

How about that! Now I remembered. Did I have to tell Gordon? Did I have to tell the ugly story of last night to him? I had to. I told him. I started with Ole Pa. It sure hurt me to remember that Ole Pa was going to die.

'The cancer is going to bite clear through him Rose-ann says. I can't bear that Ole Pa has to have such pain. Ole Pa never had a good time. He's worked all his life. Only thing beside work that he does is get shikkered and he doesn't like that any more.'

'Rose-ann is a liar,' said Gordon. 'Ole Pa won't suffer the way she says he will.'

'He won't?' I breathed deeply with gladness.

'He'll suffer. Most folk suffer. Dying, like living, isn't easy. He'll suffer, but not as Rose-ann said.'

'How come, Gordon?'

'He will be given drugs. Drugs will dull his pain. The clinic you speak of in such a scared voice is a fine place. Ole Pa couldn't go to a finer place than the clinic. You believe me?'

'I do,' I said. I believe him and I felt a might happier about Ole Pa. 'But what about—after?' I said.

'After?' Gordon didn't know what I meant. I told him about how Ole Pa got drunk and about how even when he was sober he cursed and yelled about God being an old so and so. I told Gordon that I'd never heard Ole Pa say a good thing about God and I was worried about him burning up for ever . . .

'Stop worrying so much,' Gordon told me. 'At least your grandfather believes in God, Selina. That's a good thing. Some men don't even believe there is a God.'

'But you do?'

'I do. Most certainly I do.'

'Me too,' I said. I was glad that Gordon and I both knew about God.

'I found out about God from the radio. How did you find out, Gordon?'

'From the radio? Oh! I see. Wasn't that fine. Me? How did I find out about God? First from my mother. Then from going to church.'

'I would love to go to a church,' I said.

'You would?'

'I sure would,' I said. 'And I'd sure like to feel a Bible.'

'I have a Bible.' Gordon got up and he brought me a Bible. I held the soft covered book in my hands. It was beautiful.

'I'll hold it while we talk. The preacher said the Bible was alive. Full of the living word. When I first heard that, I was young. I thought he meant jumping alive. That's not so. Is it?' I wasn't quite sure—even yet.

Gordon laughed. I didn't mind him laughing at me. His laugh was filled with love. I knew I'd been wrong about the Bible but it didn't matter.

'Is there no living word?' I asked.

'There is. Every word, and there are countless thousands, every word in the Bible is alive, Selina. Alive with truth and . . .' Gordon stopped for a moment. He moved his arm and I knew he was looking at the time. 'Selina, time is passing. We'll have a grand talk about the Bible another time. Meantime, you keep that Bible.'

I never said thank you. I hugged my very own Bible close to me. I loved that Bible.

'Tell me about last night. It isn't only Ole Pa, is it?'

'No,' I said. 'Ole Pa is only part of it.' I told how Rose-ann and Sadie were setting up their new place. That Rose-ann was tired of being put upon. I did my best to make it sound not so bad, but it sounded bad.

Gordon was quiet for so long I thought maybe he hadn't heard me. Had he fallen asleep? He'd never be so rude.

I waited and still he didn't speak. 'Gordon?' I said, and I put out my hand.

'Rose-ann must be quite a dame,' he said.

'She sure is,' I told him. I felt let down that that was all Gordon said.

'Put the whole cockeyed story out of your mind, Selina.' Gordon lit a cigarette.

'How?' I asked. How could I put it out of my mind?

'Just forget about it. Rose-ann and Sadie don't stand a chance.'

Gordon didn't know Rose-ann and Sadie.

'You don't know Rose-ann and Sadie,' I told him.

'I've known many a Rose-ann, many a Sadie. Well! Maybe not quite as low as the ladies in question, but I've known women almost as stinking low.' Now Gordon was angry. I was glad for sure. He went on and told me that there were laws to stop things like we were talking about. That a word in the right direction would send Rose-ann and Sadie scuttling. That was the word he used. I laughed at the thought of fat Rose-ann and Sadie scuttling.

I stopped laughing because I knew that the cops were the law and I knew that the cops knew all about Rose-ann and how her friends came to visit. Knew all about the little room at the end of our hall.

'The cops never stop Rose-ann,' I said. 'The cops like her.'

'What do you know! Don't worry, Selina. Don't worry about it.'

'I can't help but worry while it hangs over my head.' How could I help worrying?

'It's not hanging over your head. Not any more. Do you think I'd let a thing like this happen to you? I wouldn't let it happen to any girl in the world, let alone to you.'

Gordon sounded so all-fired certain that he could manage Rose-ann and Sadie and I believed him. I knew that nothing bad was going to happen to me. What *was* going to happen to me? I couldn't go on living with Rose-ann after she'd been stopped from starting her whore-house.

'What *is* going to happen to me?' I asked. 'I won't be able to go on living with Rose-ann, Gordon. I think she would kill me. Rose-ann hates me. You don't know her.'

Then Gordon said a wonderful thing. It wasn't what I'd wanted him to say. I'd wanted him to say: 'I'm taking care of you, Selina.' He didn't say that but he said, and I can't forget the lovely jump my heart gave as he said it: 'You,' said Gordon, 'you are going to school.'

I couldn't speak for the wonder of it. I sat and pressed my Bible into my body.

'Where did you say I was going, Gordon?' I whispered.

'To school. To a school. You are going to live there. Going to be the school's star pupil. You are going to learn so much, you can't imagine the wonderful things you are going to learn, Selina.'

'No kidding?' I whispered. I could only speak in a whisper. I was flattened with the wonder of it.

'What will I learn? Tell me.'

'I can't even begin to tell you. So many things.'

'It can't be true. But it is, isn't it? I know it is but I can't believe. I do but I can't. Can I? Can I believe it, Gordon?'

'No kidding,' Gordon laughed.

I laughed too. 'Man!' I said. 'Man!'

'Yes, man!' said Gordon. He started another cigarette. I loved the smell of the smoke. I loved everything. It was a grand world. No doubt about that.

'It's a grand world, isn't it, Gordon,' I said.

'Not bad,' said Gordon, and I heard the toothache in his voice again. I remembered he had a problem too. I knew I couldn't help any problem he had. But I could listen to it. I remembered then that he had told me his problem was really not his but mine. What had he meant?

I asked him: 'What did you mean by saying that your problem—the problem you said you had—you said it was really *my* problem? What did you mean, darling?' I'd called Gordon darling. It sounded fine. I said it again: 'Darling?'

I heard Gordon give a sigh. Oh what could it be that would make him give such a deep heavy sigh?

'Something is wrong,' I cried. 'What is it?'

'Nothing is wrong. Everything is difficult but nothing is wrong. Selina, you are going to have to trust me. Do you think you can trust me?'

Could I trust Gordon? The only thing I could trust in was Gordon.

'Of course,' I said.

'How easily you say that. Of course! Just like that! It might not be so easy.'

'Easy—so easy, so simple. You tell me what to do. Just tell me. That's all there is to it.' I snapped my fingers smartly.

'That's not all there is to it. There is more in trusting a person than doing as that person says. I want you to know that everything I do, I do only because I love you. Not only love you because you are female, a girl that I love, but because I love you as a person. A human being. A person who, if led in the right direction, could be very wonderful.'

'Me? Wonderful? Man!'

'I think you will blossom when you are moved from the dark life you live. When you are living in the sun.'

'Me? In the sun?'

'When you are helped and taught. Treated as a person.'

Not just as nothing! Treated as a person . . . me! I hugged myself at the very thought. Wasn't everything becoming a little—too too? I grew scared.

'I feel scared,' I said. 'Things are piling up. It all sounds a bit too too.'

'Don't be scared. Nothing is too too, as you say.'

'Then—everything's too hazy. Tell me more. Tell me how it's all going to happen.' I had to know more about the facts. 'Give me a few facts,' I begged.

Gordon gave a deep laugh. A short laugh.

'Of course,' he said. 'I'll give you a few facts.'

I listened to everything he said. What he said was too much to believe. I believed it though.

CHAPTER TWENTY-NINE

'If I had my way,' Gordon told me, 'I'd start things rolling at once.'

'Can't you have your way?' I asked.

'No. I must think and be careful . . .'

'Of course, of course. Yes of course,' I cried. But I wished for sure that he could have had his way.

'Firstly, I will go to a friend, a friend of mine. I will tell him about you and your life. He'll find it hard to believe me. No one could believe you've been so neglected. My friend is an important man. He will move quickly. He, not I, will take your lady mother and her plans and nip them in the bud. Don't give any thought to Rose-ann, Selina. She will be scared stiff.'

'She will?' I hoped I wouldn't be around when that happened. 'What shall we do about Ole Pa?' I asked.

'Ole Pa—we'll come to that later on.' Gordon spoke slowly and his voice was the way when I'd first heard him speak in the park: 'Can I help you?' he had asked. I'd thought it had been the tree speaking.

'I have another friend . . .' (How many friends did he have? I'd take a long shot and say maybe he had a hundred.)

'. . . a grand person. Alice Braddon is a fine person, Selina. I've known her for years. Tomorrow you are going to meet her.'

'No. Oh no. I don't want to meet her. Please, Gordon, no.' I couldn't meet one of his friends. Not a woman. Women were hard and this one would look at me and think I was a mess.

'No? Why not?' Gordon waited for me to tell him.

'She will think I'm a mess.'

'She won't. Not Alice.'

'She will. She will. She will laugh at me. At my awful clothes, my loused-up face. She will . . .'

'She won't even see you. Alice Braddon is blind, Selina.'

All the air went out of me. I couldn't even think for the wonder and strangeness. Blind! Blind, like me. In all my life I'd never thought that any other person that was blind would come my way. It would be—fine to know a blind person.

'How did she become blind?' I asked at last.

'Alice was born blind. She has always been blind.'

Born! How about that! Then Alice Braddon wouldn't even know as much as me. Wouldn't even know the colour blue or red—she would only know black. I shuddered. Poor Alice, I thought.

'How about that!' I said. 'Why I'll know more than her. How 'bout that?'

This time Gordon's laugh was long and happy.

'Why are you laughing?' I asked.

'Selina, baby—if you ever know even the half that Alice knows, I'll be so proud of you.'

I felt flattened for sure. I also felt I just might not like Alice so very much. Gordon sure thought a lot of Alice.

'You seem to think a deal of Alice,' I said, and I was surprised that my voice was so cold.

'I do. I love her.'

'Love her!' I couldn't stand that he loved her. 'How old is Alice?' I asked in the same cold voice.

'Alice! I wouldn't presume to ask her age. I'd say, yes I'd say Alice was around fifty. Yes, about fifty.'

'Man! I'm sure she's a doll.' I felt fine.

Gordon laughed again. 'She is. She is a doll. A fat wonderful dear doll. I never thought of her as a doll, but she is, for sure.' I felt that Gordon was laughing at, not with me. I didn't mind.

'Go on,' I said. 'Go on, Gordon.'

'Alice will arrange for you to enter this special school. A fine school. She will take charge of everything. It will be a new life, Selina.' Gordon started another cigarette. He was smoking too much.

'I think you smoke a little too much,' I said.

'You do? Maybe I do. Now! That's about all I think. Any more questions?'

'Exactly one million more questions,' I said. 'I want to ask you millions of things. First, Gordon, is this really happening to me. Is it? Is it really happening to me?'

'Yes.'

'I won't have to see Rose-ann any more or Sadie, if I don't want to?'

'Not if you don't want to.'

'I don't want to.'

'Then—that's that.'

'And Ole Pa will be taken care of?'

'Yes.'

It was fine trusting Gordon. I trusted him, but I asked: 'Rose-ann and Sadie really can't take me to that place?'

'They can't take you anywhere you don't want to go.'

I caught Gordon's hand and held it against my lips. I kissed his hand—quick, hurried dry little kisses.

'Oh I love you,' I cried, 'I love you. Gordon, I would have had to kill myself. The thought of going with Rose-ann and Sadie, to live in a coloured area. I thought of hundreds of black men—niggers. Thought of them standing in a line, gabbering and rattling their money. The thought of those niggers drove me but out of my mind. Black! Black men—waiting to get at me. I would have killed myself.'

Gordon got up and brought me a cold drink.

'I can imagine,' he said. Then he told me I would have to stop speaking about coloured people the way I did when I started school.

'You simply mustn't talk about people that way, Selina.'

'Mustn't I? I can't help myself. Niggers anyway aren't people . . .'

'They are, you know.'

'They are not. Ole Pa says they are apes from Africa. Ole Pa says they stink. "No stink like the bad smell of a dinge," that's what Ole Pa says and it's true. A nigger ever touched my hand, I'd cut it off—no kidding.'

'Nonsense,' said Gordon. He was getting tired. He sounded terribly tired. I loved him so much. More than ever. I reached for his hand. I couldn't find it for he had put out his cigarette and was lighting another.

'You sound tired,' I said.

'I'm not tired, Selina.'

'You sound—sad then. Are you sad? I'll try and like niggers if you want me to. I'll try for sure. It'll be hard but I'll try. But—black! Gordon, I got too much of that in my life.'

'I know that, honey.'

'I promise to try,' I said. I knew I'd never be able to do it. I could try though.

'That's fine,' said Gordon. 'That's just fine, Selina. You'll meet a deal of people from now on. People with different coloured skins, different creeds and ideas. You will have to learn.'

'I know. Don't tell me. I *know*. Tolerance.'

'I wonder if you are that smart.' He thought I couldn't learn.

'You sound like you don't believe me. Believe that I can learn to be tolerant. I can, I will. You'll see.' I couldn't bear that he didn't believe.

'*Please* believe me,' I said.

'I've been trying for years. I hope you manage better than I have.' Gordon sounded like he didn't care whether I learnt to be tolerant. Sounded as though he didn't care much about anything. He *was* tired. Suddenly the thought came to me that we'd not mentioned when and how I was to see him after I'd started my new life.

This, more than anything, I had to know. I sat for a moment and talked secretly with myself. Sometimes it's hard to talk truthfully with yourself!

From this talk I found out that I was bitterly disappointed.

If Gordon loved me, and I knew that he did, why, instead of telling me I was going to a school . . . why hadn't he said he wanted to marry me? Have me for always. It would be a test for any man to have a blind girl for a wife. It would be a test for any man to have a wife who'd always lived in a dark room on a dark street in the poor part of the city. I knew this—I also knew these things meant nothing to Gordon. Then—why?

A shocking thought came to me. Was Gordon already married?

'Are you married already, Gordon?' I hadn't meant to ask him.

'What do you mean—already?'

My face began to burn. I could have bitten out my tongue. Would he be tolerant with me?

'I mean,' I said, 'I mean, you've never said you weren't married. I thought, I was thinking, if it just happens that you *are* already married . . . then of course you couldn't marry me.' There! Would he understand, be tolerant?

He said nothing.

'Be tolerant,' I said. 'I'm sorry I asked you. I shouldn't have asked you.'

'You can ask me anything. I am not married. I've never been married.'

'Then why . . . ?'

'Why don't I ask you to marry me?'

'Not ask! Just marry. You don't have to ask.'

Once again he didn't answer me. A wall, thick and secret, grew up between us. I was on one side. Gordon on the other. I was frightened. I wanted to be with him.

'I want to be with you,' I cried. 'Everything's changing. All the happiness is fading. You've gone away.'

'No I haven't,' said Gordon. He was with me again. Maybe he'd been with me all the time. I could have been wrong!

'I felt you had gone away. I thought for sure that you had.'

My head found a nest to rest in. Found it on Gordon's shoulder. His shirt was smooth and he smelt so fine. I sniffed deeply.

'You smell so fine,' I said.

'That's nice to know.' He sat me away from him and said, 'Selina.'

I felt that I'd already started school. I sat up straight. I have a very straight back.

'Yes?' I said. 'What is it?'

'There are quite a few reasons that I haven't asked you to marry me. None of the reasons have anything to do with my not wanting to.'

'Not my being blind? Not my coming from a trash heap?'

'Lovely flowers have been known to grow out of trash heaps. Those reasons are not reasons to me.'

'Then what can they be? Tell me.' I couldn't wait to hear his reasons.

'I will. I will if you'll just hush up. It's difficult.'

'Why should it be difficult . . . I love you. You love me.'

'Love,' said Gordon, 'is only part of marriage. Important, but only a part.'

'Oh *no*.'

'But yes. Selina, I believe that destiny brings people together; sometimes it's hard to understand why. I'll use plain words. You are like a frog that has lived in a dark well. A deep dark well. Maybe meeting me was part of your destiny. The time had come for you to come out of the well. You *are* out of it. You have just wet your toes in the river of life. Haven't even wet your feet yet—just your toes.'

I wiggled my toes. They didn't feel wet. They felt cramped from my stiff shoes. Gordon went on speaking.

'I want you to wade in slowly, carefully. I want you to practise swimming in the shallows, be able to manage the currents in the river. There are currents, dangerous ones. Make no mistake about that.'

Gordon lit one of his cigarettes as though it would help him through the current he was in.

'Are you in a dangerous current now?' I asked.

'I'm used to them,' he said. I think he smiled.

'You've had some bad shocks. You've been through quite a time since we met. Last night . . .'

'Forget about last night,' I told him. 'Someone's always making with the rhubarb where I come from.'

'So it would seem,' said Gordon. 'To continue, I want you to take things slowly. I want you to have time, time to . . .'

'Yes, yes,' I said. 'Time to . . . ?'

'Time to get to know about—things. About how fine life can be. About how grand study and mastering things can be. You will find out that there are people who want to be your friends, fine people. You will be amazed!'

'Maybe I will. I hope I am. But that is not what you started out to say. It's not. Is it?'

I knew it wasn't.

'A part only. I started out to say that I want you to meet other people, women and men. I want you to get to know them. During that time I hope you'll find out various things about me. Things about my character, my habits, appearance, my family, where I come from—so many things. Things a man should tell a girl he loves about himself. Things I've had no time to tell you. How do you know there aren't things about me that you may hate—things that would shock you.'

I laughed. I laughed so much I held my stomach.

'You are but crazy,' I said. It was hard to stop laughing. Gordon wasn't laughing and I don't like to laugh alone. I stopped. 'Go on with your nonsense,' I said. I loved him, every second I loved him more than the one before. I'd think

—now I love him as much as is possible! I didn't though; my love grew and grew.

'I am not speaking nonsense. I'm telling you that I want you to know other people, other men. Then, then, Selina . . .'

'Yes? And then?'

'If after some time, after you know about other people and all about me . . .'

'Yes?'

'After that time—I'll ask you a question. If you ever, knowing me well, if you ever say: "Gordon Ralfe—time has gone by. I have learnt many things. I am older. I have met and known other men. I know all one human needs to know about another in you . . . about you . . . *and* I still love you." Selina if that time ever comes! If it ever comes . . .'

'Just how long is it going to take for me to do all this? A week? I couldn't hold out longer than a week. How long is all this hula-hula to go on?'

'Let's say a year from today.'

I was flattened. A year! A year was for ever!

'A year is for ever,' I wailed.

'A year is not for ever. Selina, you have promised to trust me! You *must* trust me. Believe that since the moment we met I've truly thought only to protect you. If I'd known how dear you were to become to me, if I'd known that. But I was not to know.'

'How could you know,' I said. 'I *have* become dear to you, and as Rose-ann always tells me, "The milk has been spilt."'

'Do we have to quote Rose-ann?' Gordon asked.

'No,' I answered, 'we don't. But it's true. You're stuck with me. I'm glad that you are.'

'Stuck with you!' Gordon said. 'That is for the future to decide. Tomorrow you will meet Alice. She'll tell you of the bright, yes bright!—your favourite word—the *bright* future that lies ahead of you . . . tell you many things you must know.'

'That'll be fine, just fine.'

'She will tell you all she knows about me. Alice knows me well.'

'So do I. So do I know you well. I love you more than anyone ever loved anyone.'

'I thought that once about a girl I was in love with. I thought I loved this girl more than anyone ever loved anyone. I found out *one* thing about this girl, and do you know, Selina, I hated that girl.'

'So do I. I hate that broad. What was wrong with her?'

Gordon laughed. His laugh made me mad.

'Don't laugh,' I said. 'You shouldn't laugh. Tell me what it was that made you hate her?'

'No,' said Gordon. 'It's a bad thing to tell one human anything you don't like about another. A very bad thing.'

'Ok.,' I said. 'But I'd sure like to know what that girl did to you.'

'I never said she *did* anything. Just there was something about her, a personal thing. It was a long time ago. Let's look more to tomorrow, to your future.'

'Yes. Will I meet Alice here?'

'I will bring her to you, in the park and leave you alone with her.'

'No, you stay.'

'I'll not be far away. If you want me, I'll be there.'

'On the bench from where you first saw me?'

'If that's what you want. Yes.'

Peace came into my heart.

Was there in the world a more thought-about girl? I didn't think so.

With the promise of tomorrow in front of me I knew I could get through the night ahead.

If only I didn't have to go back to the room—ever.

As though Gordon knew what I was thinking, he said:

'I wish I didn't have to send you back to your people.'

'Do I have to go?' I knew I had to.

'You must. Can you imagine what would happen if you were reported missing from the park? Ole Pa would know somehow, someone had taken you there. Faber would be in trouble.'

'I suppose so,' I said sadly. 'I wouldn't like to make trouble for Mr Faber.'

A fine idea came to me. 'Gordon! You could meet Mr Faber and tell him I was here with you. How 'bout that?'

'If I were found with an eighteen-year-old missing blind girl in my apartment! Selina, this place would become a nest of scorpions. There would be trouble.'

'I'll go home,' I cried. 'Scorpions are like spiders, aren't they?'

'Only worse.'

Once, I'd got a spider's web on my hands. I hadn't known what it was. I'd been sick with the clinging sticky feeling.

'Man! Let's go now,' I cried.

'We'd better be on our way. What time is Faber coming for you, honey?'

I felt sweet when Gordon called me honey.

'I like it when you call me honey. Mr Faber will come around six.'

'Then I'm going to say good-bye to you now.'

Say good-bye to me! What did he mean?

'What do you mean, say good-bye to me now?'

'It's not polite to kiss a girl in the park. You want me to kiss you good-bye, don't you?'

'Yes,' I said. 'I'd die if you didn't.'

I knew though that men did kiss girls in parks. I'd listened to hundreds of radio stories. Nearly all of them had boys and girls kissing in parks. Gordon's manners were higher—superior.

I was glad he had such fine manners. I'd have to learn to mind my own. I'd a lot to learn.

That kiss was the gentlest kiss ever given to any girl.

I'd take a long shot on that. I knew I'd always remember it. Even if I grew to be as old as for ever.

I heard him moving about the apartment doing a few things. I went to the fresh smelling bathroom and did a few things myself.

'How do I look?' I asked Gordon. I had combed my hair and washed my hands and face. My face hurt where I'd rubbed it on the towel.

'Is my face a mess?' I asked.

'Dab gently with my clean handkerchief. Here! Let me.' My scratches were bleeding a bit.

Gordon dabbed at my face with his handkerchief. 'Rose-ann,' he said, 'I do not like!'

He was very gentle but the scratches would not stop bleeding. Not much, just a little. I shouldn't have rubbed so hard with the towel.

It couldn't be helped.

'No matter,' I said, 'it can't be helped. May I keep your hanky? I'll dab at it.'

'Do that darling. Oh my *darling*.' Gordon held me against him for the quickest moment.

We went back to Park. That trip to Park was the happiest trip of my life. It seemed to be the beginning of my new life. I was happy for sure.

It was hot under the tree.

Before he left, Gordon had told me that Alice Braddon, when she came tomorrow, would have a seeing-eye dog with her. A dog named Duke.

A dog! Jesus, what next! A seeing-eye dog! I was flattened.

'I like dogs,' I had said. 'I won't be scared.'

When I was alone I thought about Alice and her dog, and how fine it would be to have my dog along too. I hoped that Mr Faber would just happen to bring Scum-dorg with him tomorrow. Alice Braddon's dog sure had a high-tone name, but I knew he wouldn't be half as dear as Scum-dorg.

Mr Faber! The beads! Hot as it was I became cold as I remembered we'd left the beads in Gordon's apartment.

How could I face Mr Faber without his beads?' I couldn't.

I must have the beads with me for Mr Faber. But—how?

If I ran quickly to the path and called to Gordon, he'd left only a short time back. Would he hear me?

I couldn't do it. I had some pride.

The park, I could hear, was crowded with people. I'd never heard so many people in the park as on this stifling summer evening. They would think the rats were after me. Would think I was a nut. I couldn't stand by a busy path and yell a name along it. How could I?

I would have to.

All my new-found *confidence* slipped away from me, as though it had never been. I was Sleena again. I began to sweat, not only from the heat, but from the bad feeling that being Sleena gave me.

I stepped carefully, sniffing, to judge where the rose garden that edged the walk ended and the walk began.

As I went, I blamed myself for being so all-fired proud, being so proud of myself and the good things coming my way, I'd forgotten about Mr Faber, my friend. Forgotten even about Ole Pa.

I should be on the walk now. I stepped forward and fell into a crazy bed of pain, fell on my face among the roses.

God! What had happened to the roses? I knew I was in the rose garden. The smell was the same.

The softness of the petals Gordon had put in my hand had changed, and were sharper by far than the nails of Rose-ann. Sharper by far.

I lay still. I listened.

It was like the day I'd waited on the stairs, hoping someone would help me down. Just as then, no one had come along the usually busy hall, so now, no one was passing near to where I lay. I hated myself, hated being a blind girl lying in a bed of roses. Even though I hated myself, I lay as still as the air about me. Hating, but not wanting to hurt myself further.

Gordon hadn't gone very far. He had been watching me from a way off, had watched and wondered what I was about. He ran to me and although he never said a word I knew it was his hands releasing me from the pain I was lying in. He led me back to the oak tree.

I was crying in a mixed-up way. Glad that he had come to me. Angry with the pain digging into my face and, most of all, that I'd become Sleena again at the the first little upset.

If a little upset like this could do it, what would I be when I got with Rose-ann again. I felt—trashy.

Gordon knelt in front of me. 'What the hell were you up to?' He sounded angry. This made me feel worse than ever.

'Don't be mad. Please don't be mad.' My crying grew louder.

'Stop. Stop the noise. I know you are hurt. I know that, honey. Gordon knows you are hurt, but stop making this noise.'

His hands gripped my shoulders, he *was* angry.

Gordon! Angry with me! I couldn't bear it. It hurt more than the pain of my face.

His anger, the heat, the pain and disappointment, being blind, rolled into a lump and struck me. I screamed. Only a small scream—but a scream.

Gordon put his hand over my mouth and a voice I knew—a fresh clear, young voice, the voice of Yanek Faber, called out.

'Leave her be. Leave Sleena be. You Goddam nigger.'

CHAPTER THIRTY

How could such a fresh boyish voice make the great world
stand still? The world stood still, then with a crazy jerk and
jolt, it began to whirl again, faster than ever before, the
speed made everyone quite crazy.

The first sound I heard was my own thin high laugh—I
laughed and called out: 'Nigger! No nigger here, man.' Both
the words and laugh were muffled by a hand held across my
mouth.

The voice had spoken of Gordon, had said Gordon was a
nigger. This I would not have. I knew that it was true, but I
would not stand for it.

The voice belonging to the hand over my mouth said:

'Not like *this*. Not *this* way.' Instead of coming from near
by, the words came from high up and far away.

I pushed away the hand and called again: 'No nigger here,
man.' I did this because the young voice kept on insisting
that there was a nigger, a goddam nigger, right here under
my tree.

The high-up, far away voice called out and the voice was
filled with distress. It didn't say much, just called a name. A
name I didn't know.

'Selina . . . Selina . . .'

I was Sleena. Who the hell was Selina? Why didn't she
answer and stop the voice? I'd call too, help the pained voice
along a bit. I yelled loudly—through my trumpet: 'Selin-
aaa . . .'

'Oh my *darling*, don't . . .' Man! Someone was in trouble!

Somehow, Sadie got right inside of me. I struggled to keep
her out but she's a strong one, that Sadie, she slays you.

'*Wah!*' she yelled. 'I told you—wah! He's *got* you . . .
wahhh . . .'

Sadie and I fought and struggled. I got rid of her.

Tired! I was but tired. No chance of taking it easy though.
No sooner had I rid myself of Sadie than Rose-ann took her

137

place. She *had* got fat. Filled me up. I could hardly draw breath.

I never heard Rose-ann laugh so crazy as she did from inside of me.

'Har har har—a har har har. Oh Jeez! Har har har. I'm but slayed. Sleena loves a nigger . . .'

'No. No, no, no,' I screamed. 'I hate black things.'

Much harder getting rid of Rose-ann than Sadie. I managed though.

Man! What a rhubarb! I lay on the ground and wondered what it was all about. Why was I lying on the ground? Was it the ground? Ole Pa thumped again and again.

Now what had that young voice said? Something about a black man. No. I was mixed up. Rose-ann it was. Rose-ann had told me, '. . . a swell apartment in the coloured area . . .'

Coloured! Black! Name of God, no. I was in the swell apartment. The hands touching me were the hands of a coloured man. Name of God, no.

'No,' I screamed. 'Get your hands off of me. You black, you goddam nigger.' I fought. Man, how I fought.

'Don't—do—this—to—me . . . Selina . . .' There! My oak *could* talk. I'd always known it could. But who was it talking to, who was Selina?

'Why don't you answer the tree, Selina, it's not often one sees a heart-shaped tree,' I yelled out through my trumpet. Loud! It was loud.

'Oh my *God*,' prayed the tree. It was sad because Selina wouldn't answer it.

The powerful young voice kept on—it had never stopped: 'Help . . . help . . . Here, in *here!* Under the tree . . . Coloured man . . . Help, *white* girl . . . Help, help, she's bleeding . . . Hurry, hurry . . .'

Footsteps came running. From all over the park, pounding over the grass—coming to the rescue—coming to attack? *That* was more likely.

I didn't like the sounds they were making. Who were these people? Men, women, even children. Yelling and panting.

Sounded bad for sure. I'd never heard such a crazy mob. Had I? I had. Many a time on the radio, an inflamed mob.

This was not the radio, this was for real. Man! I hoped they weren't after me. Me? I was but crazy. They were out to catch the black man.

'Here . . . in here . . . under the tree . . . Help!' I called to them.

Things too too—are dangerous. I crawled against the tree. Good! I'd stick close to the tree until the storm was over.

Man! It was a bad storm. Would it never end?

What was it all about? I didn't know. Did anyone know?

'What's it all about?' I called.

No one had time to answer the questions of a blind girl. There had been someone once who'd answered my questions. Who had it been?

I remembered.

Gordon! Where was Gordon? What was happening under our tree? A dreadful thing . . . Where was Gordon?

I listened to the heavy breathing of struggling men. The sounds of high-pitched and of low-muttering voices, to the dreadful sound of hatred.

The dreadful sound of hatred.

A voice trumpeted above the others:

'The sonofabitch is getting away. Don't let him get away . . .'

Then, I was alone under the tree.

Voices grew fainter, as pounding feet chased away after the coloured man.

The man that was—Gordon. Name of God, no!

Madness and the shock that had caused the madness left me. I stood up and called:

'Oh *God*. Take care of him. Let him get away from us.'

Just let him get away. Nothing else mattered. Nothing but that Gordon escape.

What had he done to make it so that he had to escape? Nothing. Gordon had done nothing.

If his mother, the mother that bore him—if his father—if they had been white people, this wouldn't be happening. Gordon could have stayed, faced the people, told what had happened. Such a simple thing. A blind girl had fallen among the rose bushes and scratched her face.

A simple thing! But his parents had been coloured, born with dark skins. He'd had no say in the matter. Like me being blind. I'd had no say in the matter.

My blindness hadn't turned Gordon against me. My fate had deepened his love for me.

'Oh my darling,' I moaned, and pressing cold hands against my heart I felt the broken pieces of the cup he had filled with happiness. Felt the small jagged bits cut at my inside. I'd never known such pain.

Yanek Faber burst back under the tree. In his sweet high voice he told me: 'He got away, Sleena. He got away. Don't worry—he's all bloodied up—he won't get far. Jeepers! He knows how to fight, that nigger . . .'

'Keep still,' I told him. 'Keep quiet.'

'You feeling bad, Sleena? You look bad.'

'I'm fine,' I said. 'Just keep quiet.'

He sat quietly. Yanek, Mr Faber's boy.

I heard the muffled sounds of the returning crowd.

No pounding footsteps; slow, disappointed.

Soon I knew, the mob that because of my ignorance, my intolerance, I belonged to would be with me.

Full of questions, full of excitement. Well, let them come. We sat waiting.

I remembered hearing Gordon call: 'You are destroying me, Selina . . .' He had been *wrong!*

The strength, so a part of him, would help him over this . . .

It was me, Selina, I had destroyed.

There was sorrow in the slow movement of branches above my head, in the pulsing silence of the ground beneath me.

I put my hand over the burial ground of my music-box. I'd never asked Gordon the words of the tired little song.

'Are you studying French, Yanek?' I whispered.

'I know a little.' He sounded surprised.

'What are the words: il pleut, il pleut?' I asked.

'It is raining, raining, I think.'

'Thank you,' I said. 'Thank you.'

'Why, Sleena?'

'Hush,' I told him. 'Please hush.'

I began to weep. I sat and wept. It was fitting that I should.

I wept for the blindness of my heart and mind; for my intolerance; and my meaningless, cheap hatred—hatred of a thing that didn't rate hatred.

I wept bitterly, and I knew with terror that I would cry more, and more bitterly later, for I would never hear or be with Gordon again.

He had gone. Had been shamefully, and like a mad dog, chased away. I knew—sure as I knew God—that (and this was my greatest pain of all) I knew that Gordon would keep me from falling back into the dark well he had lifted me out of. He would send Alice Braddon into my life the way he had planned. I knew this and it hurt more than death could ever hurt.

Hot coals of fire upon my 'pale gold head.'

Surely weeping such as this would squeeze tears out of me? I felt my face. No tears.

'You O.K., Sleena?'

'Fine. Just fine, Yanek.'

I stopped crying and straightened my back. 'My name is not Sleena, Yanek. My name is *Selina*,' I told him.

Soon the crowd would be upon me. I didn't mind.

How strange it was. How very strange. All my life I'd hated black, hated it so much and yet—beautiful people in my life had been coloured . . .

Gordon. His brother Paul and—and . . .

As the group of interested excited people gathered about me, I remembered and I called . . .

'Pearl. I'm sorry Pearl . . .'

'She's in shock,' said a stranger's voice. 'Poor kid's in shock.'

'. . . and do you wonder?' said another.

Let them talk. Let them wonder. It didn't matter. Nothing really mattered, for I knew that I would never hear the sounds of bells and drums. Bells and drums sounded for a pure-hearted girl. To my grief I knew this, but . . .

A tiny ray of light lightened my darkness. The smallest beginning of, could it be—hope—was born in my heart.

Couldn't I, Selina, beat a drum, ring a clear-sounding bell for someone else—for something?

Could I?

And if I could, then for whom? For what?

There must be someone—something?

Man! I was but tired. Too tired to search, to think.

Suddenly a bright all-seeing light flamed up. Flooded my mind, bathed me in its beauty. How could I have forgotten? —How could I?

Gordon's favourite word, a 'something' that even he had been unable to master.

Tolerance!

I heard the first soft beat of drum, my drum.

I stood up and I called out, clearly, loudly, like the sound of a bell almost:

'Pearl, I love you, Pearl . . .' And I did.

'She's in a bad way, for sure,' said one of the strange voices.

4 Thrilling Bestsellers by Thomas B. Costain...
Packed with Love and Intrigue, Passion and Power

CONQUERING FAMILY
Unforgettable drama of a powerful family who sought to sweep the whole world before them. 352 pgs. "Fascinating," N.Y. Times.

MAGNIFICENT CENTURY
Costain vividly recreates the turbulent and passionate era of Henry III. 383 pgs. "Magnificent," N.Y. Herald Tribune.

CONQUERING FAMILY

"Costain has brought all the skill of a prime storyteller. He riots amid the actual happenings in perhaps the most richly dramatic and romantic country we know...A thrilling narrative."—Salt Lake City Tribune.

THREE EDWARDS

"So colorful and gusty is his style, so filled with phrases that grip and hold, no fiction he ever wrote holds the breathless interest of the reader more tightly."—Miami Herald.

MAGNIFICENT CENTURY

"Fascinating...thoroughly enjoyable...history at its best...written by a man who combines a love of his subject matter with an understanding of the all-too-often overlooked fact that history—accurate, factual history—is the most fascinating tale of all."—San Francisco Chronicle

MAIL ATTACHED COUPON NOW ⟶